CRASH & BURN

Into The Fire Series

J.H. CROIX

This is a work of fiction. Names, characters, businesses, places, events and incidents are either the products of the author's imagination or used in a fictitious manner. Any resemblance to actual persons, living or dead, or actual events is purely coincidental.

ISBN: 9781794194830

Cover design by Cormar Covers

Cover Photography: Wander Aguiar

Cover models: Zack Salaun & Adrea McNulty

❀ Created with Vellum

"This is love: to fly toward a secret sky, to cause a hundred veils to fall each moment. First, to let go of life. Finally, to take a step without feet." -Rumi

Sign up for my newsletter for information on new releases & get a FREE copy of one of my books!

http://jhcroixauthor.com/subscribe/

Follow me!
jhcroix@jhcroix.com
https://amazon.com/author/jhcroix
https://www.bookbub.com/authors/j-h-croix
https://www.facebook.com/jhcroix
https://www.instagram.com/jhcroix/

Chapter One

RACHEL

"Henry!"

My dog, the aforementioned Henry, had just bolted away from me. I picked up my jog to a flat-out run, mud splashing on my face as one of my feet slammed into a puddle.

"Dammit, Henry," I muttered to myself.

Ahead of me on the trail, he looked back, covered in mud, with his long tail wagging back and forth. I couldn't help but laugh. I loved my dog, but he was nuts. Black and gold with silky fur, he was full of energy and adventure.

We were taking one of our usual runs. Now that it was early spring, or rather mud season, as it was best known in Alaska, it was warm enough to get outside more often. For a moment, I thought Henry was done with his fun, but he looked away and kept on running, appearing to think this was a game.

"Henry!"

At this rate, he would probably make it all the way back to the car before I caught up to him.

That's fine. I need more exercise anyway. My ass is big enough already.

Coming around the corner on the trail, I let out a yelp when I almost collided with someone. My feet skidded in the mud, and I fell into an inglorious heap.

"Ouch!" I exclaimed as my knee collided with a rock somewhere in the mud.

Rising up slightly on my hands, I glanced down at my muddy legs and shirt. I'd fallen in the edge of a puddle and was now soaked and covered in muck. When I looked up, my gaze ran smack into Remy Martin. "Oh shit."

Of course I said that out loud.

You see, Remy was sexy as hell. At the moment, he happened to be wearing a pair of running shorts that molded to his legs, which were nothing but muscle. *He* was nothing but muscle.

My eyes traveled up his legs and across his muscled chest. His heather gray T-shirt was damp with sweat and conveniently—as far as my eyes were concerned, that is—delineated every muscle of said sexy chest. When my gaze traveled to his face, mossy green eyes met mine, his dark blond hair mussed. Although his skin had a light sheen of sweat, he appeared barely winded.

"Oh shit?" he asked after staring at me for a moment. "Are you mad at me for existing?"

His slow southern drawl slid over me. Remy's voice was like honey and whiskey—rich with a hint of sweet, and so damn sexy. Just hearing him speak sent heat spinning through me.

Fuck. This time, I kept my profanity to myself. I was sitting here, covered in mud, with the hottest man in town staring down at me. I felt my cheeks heating and was relieved I had mud on my face because perhaps it would obscure my blush. Score one for mud.

"I was mad at the puddle, not you," I replied, only half-lying. I *was* mad at the puddle, but I was also horrified to be in this state in his presence.

With a shake of my head, I moved to scramble to my

feet. I managed to get halfway up and then my foot slid out from under me again. Because it was *that* kind of day.

Remy held a hand out, and I bit my lip with a sigh. Reaching up, his strong grip curled around my hand as he pulled me up easily. Once I was upright, he stepped back, making sure I was fully out of the puddle and on firmer ground before he released me.

His eyes coasted over me. "Are you okay?"

Embarrassed, flustered, and annoyed as hell at my body's swift reaction to Remy's presence, I managed to nod. "I'm fine, just a little dirty. Thanks for helping me up," I said with a wry smile, gesturing at the mud streaks on my legs.

Remy's mouth kicked up at one corner in a half-grin. Sweet hell, his grins should be illegal. My lower belly clenched and heat radiated outward.

"Anytime, darlin'," he replied, his grin stretching to the other side of his mouth. "I presume that was your dog who just ran past me?" One of his brows hitched up.

I had completely forgotten about Henry. That just went to show how easily Remy rattled me. "Yes, oh God, I need to catch up to him."

As I started to turn, Remy put his hand on my elbow. Before I could say a word, he spoke. "Wait."

The word was low, and somehow authoritative. But then, everything about Remy was powerful and authoritative. Oh, and sexy as hell. Did I mention that yet?

The man practically dripped sex with his southern drawl, his fit, muscled body, and his dangerously heated gaze. To top it all off—nature really had been too generous with him—he had chiseled features, high cheekbones, and full lips. The man could've been a model. Yet, he seemed oblivious to his effect on women. He was always gracious and polite.

I had two conflicting impulses whenever I was near Remy. I wanted to throw myself at him. And, I wanted to curl up in his arms and be held, to have his strength wrapped around me. Remy was that kind of man, the kind you knew would save you if you needed saving.

Before I even had a chance to ask why Remy wanted me to wait, Henry appeared, dashing toward us and stopping right in front of Remy. Looking down at him, I couldn't help but laugh. "*Of course* you come when I'm not even calling."

Henry wagged his entire body, practically vibrating when Remy dropped his hand from my elbow and knelt down to pet him. Remy didn't seem to care one bit that Henry was covered head to toe in mud and was licking his face all over. Even my dog liked Remy.

When Remy straightened, Henry circled around my legs, and I reached down to pet him. It didn't matter if he got mud on me because I was already covered in it. I looked over at Remy. "Thanks again for helping me up."

Remy smiled, his gorgeous green eyes crinkling at the corners. "Anytime, darlin'." He was quiet for a beat, his gaze considering. "You sure you're okay?"

"I'm fine. Just in serious need of a shower." Leaning down, I clipped Henry's leash on his collar. He didn't usually dash off, but I preferred to keep him close until we were back in my car. "Thanks again," I said with a wave as I started to walk. When I took a step, sharp pain shot from my knee. A gasp hissed through my teeth when I paused.

Remy was back at my side in a flash. "I'll walk you back."

"Oh my God, I can walk, Remy. I banged my knee when I fell. It's no biggie," I insisted.

He ignored me and stepped to the side where Henry was, taking the leash from me and sliding his other hand into the crook of my elbow. "I can't let you walk back alone. The last thing I want is for you to slip and fall again."

I wanted to argue, but I sensed Remy was going to walk with me, whether I argued the point or not. "Fine," I muttered.

We didn't have far to go. Within a few minutes, we reached the parking lot at the base of the trail. I let Henry into the back of my car, and he immediately started lapping up water from his travel bowl.

Remy grinned. "Smart," he said, gesturing to the towels layered on the carpet in the back of my small SUV.

"Oh, I'm always prepared for Henry to get dirty." I closed the back of the SUV when Henry curled up and rested his chin on his paws, checking to make sure the windows in the back were cracked open.

I turned to look at Remy, and caught him taking a nice, long look at my ass. Heat rushed to my cheeks, yet somehow, I didn't mind. Seeing as I considered him eye candy, I guessed it was fair play for him to check me out. I couldn't resist commenting though.

"Were you just staring at my ass?"

Chapter Two

REMY

Rachel Garrett was all kinds of trouble. She might as well have had the word tattooed on her forehead as far as I was concerned. Although, a more appropriate place for the tattoo in question would be on the swell of her breasts. Precisely where I tended to have trouble with my wandering eyes.

With her dark brown hair, flashing blue eyes, and curves for days, Rachel was downright sexy. Her sharp attitude only made her more appealing. In short, she was *my* kind of woman. This was certainly not the first time I had noticed her. I'd been living in Willow Brook for close to a year now, having moved to town after taking a position as a hotshot firefighter on a crew here.

I crossed paths with Rachel every so often through the connections of shared friends. Yet, I'd never been alone with her before. Just now, she had mud splattered on her face, all over her legs, on her arms, and smudging her shirt and shorts. All I could think was that mud wrestling with Rachel would be more than fun.

I was a gentleman though. I was also legitimately

concerned she hurt herself when she almost collided with me and slipped in the mud.

"Were you just staring at my ass?" she asked.

Caught red-handed. I had, in fact, been staring at Rachel's ass. I didn't care to try to hide it and let my eyes linger just a bit longer. She had a plump, luscious bottom. With her shorts wet and molded to her body, her curves were outlined perfectly for me.

I was no misogynistic jerk. I didn't really think they were outlined for *me*, but my body sure thought so. I drank in the sight of her, my gaze coasting over the luscious curve of her ass, then to her breasts, where her nipples were visible through the fabric of her damp T-shirt and bra.

When my eyes finally reached her face, her cheeks were flushed and her eyes were flashing.

"Yes, I was," I drawled.

Despite the mud on her cheeks, I could still see her flush deepen. The air around us felt electric as Rachel stared at me. I didn't doubt for one second just how fiery Rachel would be tangled up with me.

I hadn't been interested in a woman in too damn long. I was no monk, but I could've been confused for one the last few years of my life. I shook my thoughts away from that path.

Rachel's mouth dropped open and then she snapped it shut before putting a hand on her hip and glaring at me. Little did she know that seeing her angry only sent a hot jolt of lust through me.

"Well, that was rude," she sputtered, lifting her arm and wiping the back of her hand across the mud on her cheek, an entirely pointless attempt to clean her face, especially considering her hand was covered in mud too.

A low chuckle escaped from me, and her eyes flashed again. Stepping closer, she actually wagged her finger in my face. "That's not funny."

"Darlin', you're covered in mud and you're gorgeous. I shouldn't have laughed though, so my apologies."

Yet again, her mouth opened and snapped shut.

"How's your knee?" I added.

She flexed it and shrugged. "It's fine." Then, she put her palm on my chest and gave me a little shove.

Damn, the feel of her palm against my chest was like a hot brand right through my shirt. I didn't even think, I covered her hand with mine and stepped closer. Nothing was funny now.

I wanted to kiss her. Sweet hell, did I want to kiss her. But I wouldn't. Not now. "Let's just be honest. I want you. I'll let you think on that."

At that, I released her hand and stepped back. Henry, her goofy dog, stuck his nose to the crack in the window at that moment, giving out a low woof. Rachel looked at Henry and then back at me, her blue eyes darkening. "I have to go," she said abruptly.

"You do that, sweetheart."

Chapter Three

REMY

I kicked a chair away from the table with my boot, slipping into it and nodding when Ward Taylor called over a greeting. "Hey, Remy."

Ward turned back to finish saying something to Cade Masters, who was seated beside him. I'd come to join a mix of crewmembers at Wildlands Lodge, all of us hotshot firefighters based out of Willow Brook, Alaska. Wildlands was a world-class lodge for all things outdoors, situated on the pristine waters of Swan Lake. It was also a local favorite bar and restaurant. Swan Lake was the centerpiece of Willow Brook, a massive lake with a stunning view of the wilderness on its far shore, the mountains beyond, and encircled with a variety of hunting and fishing lodges.

A waitress paused beside me, glancing down with a friendly smile. "What can I get for you, Remy?" she asked.

"Just the house draft on tap."

"Nothing to eat?"

"I'll take a burger," a voice called from behind me. Glancing back, I saw Beck Steele approaching the table.

Beck flashed me a grin as he slipped into the chair beside me.

"Ditto," I replied when the waitress glanced back to me.

She jotted down our orders and hurried away. I leaned back in my chair, scanning the bar while Beck greeted everyone else at the table. Considering a few of Rachel's friends were here tonight, I idly wondered if I would see her here tonight.

Rachel Garrett had done the impossible—she'd damn near set up house in my brain. I hadn't been able to stop thinking about her since I'd seen her, nor had I thought I'd ever care enough about anyone again. Sometimes life throws curveballs you can't anticipate, and the wreckage afterwards is strewn so thoroughly across the landscape of your life, all you can do is pick up stakes and move.

That's what I'd done. I'd been a firefighter in western North Carolina, where I was born. Once my life skidded sideways for reasons entirely out of my control, I headed to hotshot training in California. As soon as a position opened up here in Willow Brook, I took it.

There were quite a few things I missed about home, but I didn't view my choice to move away as running. There'd been nothing left to run from. I found a change of scenery didn't hurt so much. Yet, I'd come here knowing no one could ever get through to my heart again.

Rachel had somehow slipped right through, knocking loose a few bricks in the walls around my heart. Those walls had simply built themselves. When you lost just about everyone who matters, sometimes that happened. Or that's what I told myself, time and again.

Turning when someone else said my name, I found Jesse Franklin looking at me expectantly. "Yeah?"

"I was wondering if you were going to be able to be on duty over Memorial Day weekend. It's a busy time around here, and it seems like half the station's going on vacation."

"I'll be here. Just tell me where you need me to be."

"Sweet," Jesse replied with a grin and a wink.

"You're from North Carolina, right? Do you get down there to visit your family much?" Charlie, Jesse's wife, asked. They'd up and gotten married only recently, although they'd been together over a year. Or, at least, that was what I'd pieced together. Charlie was pretty, with dark glossy hair and gray eyes. She was also damn smart and a good doctor, which I know from personal experience. Firefighting had its challenges, including minor and major injuries. Over the winter, a beam had fallen when I was on my way out of a house, one of the heavy nails slicing through the side of my hand and leaving a crooked scar for my trouble. Charlie had stitched it up as neatly as possible.

I imagined she was being polite by asking about me visiting my family. It was a perfectly normal question. My chest tightened, but I breathed through the heartbeat of pain and shook my head. "Can't say that I do. Both my parents passed away."

Charlie's eyes widened and then a look of clear understanding passed across her face. "I'm so sorry, Remy. I didn't know," she replied, her tone warm and soft.

The sharp ache in my heart was easing. I was used to it by now. "You couldn't have known," I said. I had to steel myself every time I thought about my parents. Life could be fucking cruel.

A vacation on the Gulf Coast. A tornado in the darkness. A single street and three houses. My parents and four other people gone. Just like that.

All that was left of my family were me and my little sister, Shay. Shay was closer to home, and I missed her. The only reason I didn't worry about her was because the biggest threat to her was finally locked up in jail. I shook my thoughts away, sensing Charlie's eyes lingering on me, the concern in her gaze deepening.

Around us, conversation carried on with joking, laughter from a game of pool nearby, the sound of glasses clinking, and lives simply carrying on. All the while, I felt like there were gaping holes in my heart I didn't know if I could ever repair.

Charlie rested her hand on my arm, her touch cool and soft. "I know what it's like to lose someone you love. My father and my sister died. I know. Time helps."

I took a breath, holding her eyes. "Time does help. Thank you," I managed through the tightness in my throat.

Someone else said my name, snapping through the temporary lull between Charlie and me. Her kindness almost made me hurt more. She gave my forearm a little squeeze and then her hand wrapped around her wine glass as she took a sip, looking away. I sensed she knew I needed to move on from this moment, and I wanted to thank her for that too.

I searched out the voice that had called my name, my eyes landing on Beck. He was always quick with a joke and rock solid out in the field. "Yes?" I replied, ignoring the pain in my heart.

"Oh, I was just asking if you bet any in the pool for the Ice Classic," Beck explained.

"What the hell is that?" I countered, relieved to latch onto something.

Beck's grin widened as Levi Phillips leaned forward beside him. Levi was just as much the jokester as Beck, and the two of them tended to take turns.

"Every year, it's a bet on when the ice will crack on the river," Levi explained.

"A bet on when the damn ice cracks? What the hell, boys?"

Before I left that night, I'd been persuaded into betting fifty bucks on the silliest thing I'd ever heard of.

A bit later, I stepped out of the bar, pausing halfway across the parking lot behind Wildlands. The early spring air still had a bite of cold, but it contained a hint of earthiness to it. It smelled like mud and leaves with nothing more than a promise of the green to come. I took several deep breaths, my mind spinning back to what spring was like in the mountains of North Carolina when I was a boy.

Spring there wasn't quite as powerful as it was here, yet that same sense of quickening in the air and the pungency of everything melting and slowly unfurling from the frost was vivid in my memory.

Fuck. I kicked that memory to the curb in my mind. It was too tangled up in the loss of my parents. I missed them, missed them like hell. I missed Shay too. Yet, she was the one who had talked me into becoming a firefighter in the first place and had encouraged me to move to take this position. Her heart was big as the sky, and she was so open in spite of everything.

She had more pain to carry than I did, more reason not to trust in life, in the world, and in the vagaries of faith. Yet, she still did. She was a living, breathing example of the concept of hope. She called me just this morning and left a silly message on my voicemail.

I made my way to my truck and climbed in. After starting the engine and pulling out onto Main Street in downtown Willow Brook, I tapped the speaker button on the screen in the dashboard, pulling up Shay's number. It would be late there, but she would answer. She always did.

Shay picked up on the second ring. "Hey, big brother," she said with a laugh.

"Hey, sis, how you doing?"

Joy spun around my heart. There were a few spots of joy in my life the last few years. My sister was one of them.

"I'm good."

"You all settled in?" I asked.

"Of course I am. It's not like I'm living alone, Remy. I just got to the farm yesterday. Ash is out of town for the month, but Jackson's here. You know he won't let a hair on my head get hurt."

My heart gave a painful *thud*. "I know."

Shay had been to hell and back in the last year with her asshole of an ex, who was finally fucking in jail for what he put her through. By some miracle, she was still joyful. After she made it through to the other side, her spirit had shined its light again.

I'd all but badgered her into moving in with my old buddy from back home and his younger sister, who happened to be a good friend of Shay's as well. I hadn't wanted her to live alone. I worried too much.

"I don't know why you're so concerned. I've got Jackson to boss me around just as much as you do. You don't need to worry about me anymore, Remy. I swear."

"And you don't need to tell me not to worry."

Shay's answering laugh was low. "Fine then. Tell me how you're doing. Is it spring there yet?"

"Well, since we talked just yesterday, there's a little bit less snow on the ground today and it's getting muddier."

She laughed again. "Right, but you said things melt fast there once they start."

"That I did, sis."

"Hang on a sec," she said. Her voice was muffled as she said something to someone in the background. I looked ahead as I turned, and a car came into view on the side of the road. Shay's voice came back on. "Sorry about that."

"No problem. I gotta go. There's a car on the side of the road. I'm gonna check and make sure they're okay."

"Of course you are. You take care of everybody, Remy. I love you."

"Love you too, sis. I'll talk to you soon."

After I ended the call, I slowed, pulling up behind the car, its hazard lights blinking in the darkness. I turned on my own hazards before I climbed out. Walking to the driver's side of the car, I rapped my knuckles against it, thinking the SUV looked familiar.

When the window rolled down, I found myself looking into Rachel's bright blue eyes, the dim light inside the car reflecting off her glossy brown hair. The moment my eyes met hers, a jolt of need hit me. That was how much this girl got to me.

Chapter Four

REMY

"Remy?"

"That would be me, sweetheart. Is something wrong with your car?"

Rachel looked away and then leaned her head back against the seat, her eyes sliding sideways to mine again. "I think I have a flat. I just pulled over. I was about to call someone."

"You *think* you have a flat?"

"Well, my front right tire was making a whooshing sound. Trust me, I wanted to keep going, but it didn't seem like the smartest move."

"Let me check," I called over my shoulder as I rounded the front of her car. Sure enough, in the soft glow of the blinking hazard lights, I could see her front tire was flat.

I hadn't realized Rachel had gotten out of the car to follow me around until I straightened and turned back, promptly colliding with her. It was a dark, cold night. Although technically it was spring, most people would consider it winter by the weather rather than the date. When I bumped against Rachel's lush body, I became instantly aware of her full breasts pressed against my chest. For a flash, I could even feel her taut nipples through the fabric of her shirt.

Hot damn. *This* woman. The last thing that should've been on my mind was kissing her, and yet my eyes fell straight to her full, luscious lips. All I could wonder was what they would feel like underneath mine.

She stepped back quickly. "Sorry," she said, her voice raspy.

The other night, when I'd been thinking about Rachel— because Rachel had burrowed into my mind—I thought her voice was like sex, always slightly husky with a rough edge to it.

"No need to apologize. I was just saying you were right. Your tire's definitely flat. I'll change it for you."

"Oh. You will?"

I dragged my eyes away from her sweet lips and nodded. "Of course I will, sweetheart. Do you have a spare?"

"Uh-huh." She spun away quickly, hurrying to the back of her car. It was a compact vehicle, one of those small SUV's with the spare tire mounted on the back.

I followed her, waiting as she opened the hardcover case where the spare was stored.

"You'd think I would know how to change a tire. I don't," she said, glancing to me with a sheepish smile curling the corners of her mouth.

"No worries. I've changed plenty of tires, sweetheart."

Rachel stared at me for a few beats. I could've sworn her cheeks flushed, although it was dark and the light from the hazards was barely there. I reminded myself I was there to help her change her damn tire. Not kiss her senseless, no matter how much I wanted a taste of her.

"I'm sure you have. I don't like to be that girl, but I'll just let you take over. I don't even know how to get the tire out of here," she said, gesturing to the case.

I pulled my phone out of my pocket, tapping the flashlight button and handing it to her. "Hold that. Please," I added.

"Sure thing."

She held it up, allowing me to see the small bag of tools right where they should be in a waterproof bag inside the container. I got to work, unscrewing the tire from where it was held in place, snagging the jack and going around to the front of her car.

I had it taken care of, right quick. The only thing slowing me down was Rachel wanted to know everything I was doing. There I was, kneeling on the ground, with her hovering over my shoulder. Not that I minded her proximity, not even a little. It's just she had me hard as a rock, and I was trying to change a fucking tire, for crying out loud.

"So, what's that?" she asked for about the twentieth time.

"This?" I replied, holding up the lug wrench.

"Uh-huh. Does every car have those?"

"Sure do, sweetheart. Every basic car has a spare, with a jack and this for unscrewing the lug nuts ."

I quickly tightened the lugs on her spare tire. I had tested it to make sure the pressure was good before we put it on. I'd been slightly disappointed I couldn't tell her it wasn't. Now, I didn't have an excuse to give her a ride home.

"Wow. Learn something new every day. Now I know how to change a tire," she said, when I moved to ease the jack down.

"It's a handy thing to know," I offered as I stood, adjusting my jeans in the process.

My cock, oblivious to the fact this was not a convenient time to be lusting after Rachel, was pressing against my zipper.

I straightened, dusting my hands on my jeans, and her head bumped into my shoulder. Lifting my gaze, I found her eyes right there, inches away from mine. Rachel was compact and curvy, the kind of woman I could imagine lifting up easily, letting her wrap her legs around my waist while I buried myself inside of her.

Time froze. Well, freeze wasn't quite the right word to describe what time did. Rather, everything around us stopped for a weighted moment and then suddenly felt electrified. She stared at me, her lips parting and her tongue darting out to swipe across her bottom lip.

Reason fled the building, thought hot on its heels. Desire bolted to the forefront. Before I could stop myself, I straightened further, lifting a hand and brushing away a lock of hair that had fallen across her eyes.

My hand moved on its own, tucking her hair behind her ear and feeling the goose bumps rising under my fingertips along the soft, downy skin of her neck. Then, I dipped my head. Because I *had* to kiss her.

The moment my lips met hers, the air sizzled around us, need racing like fire through my veins. Her lips were soft and warm, a contrast to the chilly air around us. I brushed my lips across hers once, twice, and then again. Drawing back the barest distance, I asked, "Sweetheart, do you want this kiss?"

I could feel the soft puff of her breath. I ignored the lust whipping at me and waited. I knew what I wanted, but I needed to know she wanted the same thing.

"Yes," she breathed, that single word of assent sending another jolt of lust through me.

This time, when our lips met, the flame spun around us, catching us in its center. Another brush of my lips against hers, and then I dove into the warm sweetness of her mouth when she moaned into mine.

Threading my hand in the silky fall of her hair, I turned, caging her in my arms and pressing her against the car. She kissed like a dream, soft and sweet. She tasted like honey and smelled like sugar. Her tongue slicked against mine and her hand slid up my back as she flexed into me. Her body was soft, lush, and generous.

I lost my goddamn mind kissing Rachel on the side of the road in the darkness.

She threw herself into the kiss just as deeply as I did. It was hot and fast, slow and sensuous, and then it went deep, wild, and wet. It was all of that and more.

My hand slid down her side, into the dip of her waist, over the curve of her hip, and around to cup her sweet ass. I let out a growl when she arched into me as I rocked my arousal into the cradle of her hips.

Suddenly, lights flashed across us as a car came around the corner. I'd forgotten everything — everything but her.

I gentled our kiss, not quite ready to break our connection, but knowing I needed to soon. Reluctantly, I eased away slowly. I leaned my head back to look at the stars above before looking back to her. "Sweetheart, your kiss is like honey."

Rachel laughed softly. Although I couldn't see it, I knew her cheeks flushed pretty and pink. "And you kiss like a handsome devil," she countered.

"I'll follow you home," I said, as I stepped back from her.

The car was now definitely close enough to see us. Not that I cared one iota if someone saw me kissing Rachel on the side of the road in the dark, and practically manhandling her. But I had some respect, and I wasn't so sure she wanted to be seen in that position. I might not have lived in Willow Brook that long, but I knew small towns well enough to know whoever was driving down the road right now likely knew one, if not both, of us.

"Follow me home? You don't need to do that."

As if to prove my last thought, the vehicle slowed to the side of the road where we were parked, and the window rolled down. "I thought that was your truck, Remy. Oh hey, Rachel," Beck commented, looking past me to her. "Everything okay?"

Rachel and I were now standing with a good six inches

between us. My body protested the distance, and I ignored it.

"I had a flat tire, and Remy changed it for me," Rachel replied. "Now he says he's going to follow me home. Don't you think that's a little silly?"

Beck smiled, his teeth flashing white in the darkness. "No. Spare tires are finicky. Damn miracle your spare wasn't flat itself. I don't even need to ask Remy if he checked it before he put it on."

Rachel's gaze shifted to me.

"Of course I did."

"Exactly. Well, I got to get on home. Maisie's waiting for me. I got a baby to put to bed. She's been dealing with her all evening," he explained.

"Night, man," I called as he waved and drove off.

Rachel looked as if she wanted to say something more, but she didn't. She turned to walk around her car.

"Sweetheart, what's that?"

She swung back around. "What?"

"I think you were about to say something."

Rachel narrowed her eyes and then threw her head back with a laugh. "Maybe, but you just guaranteed I won't now."

With that, she spun back around, and I enjoyed the sight of her hips swinging and her sweet ass before she rounded the front of her car.

I followed her home through the darkness. It was only a few minutes, and Rachel filled my thoughts every single second of those minutes.

It had been three long years since my parents' death tore a hole through my life and left my heart half-alive. I didn't laugh often lately, not the way I laughed with Rachel. It wasn't that I couldn't crack a joke. Hell, that was easy when you were just hanging with friends. Old habits die hard, and all that.

The few passing interactions I'd had with Rachel reminded me of joy. She brought little bursts of it into my life and made my heart remember that maybe there was a reason to keep on kicking. Don't mistake that for me saying I wanted to die. It was just I felt weary to my bones. First, there'd been my parents' death and then my sister nearly fell apart at the hands of a dangerous man.

Rachel was something else, something slightly dangerous to my sanity and so delicious, I couldn't stay away. I wanted her, so damn badly I'd kissed her like a fool on the side of the road. Yet, she stirred deep waters.

I followed the soft glow of her tail lights along the dark highway, wondering where she would lead me.

Chapter Five

RACHEL

My hands were shaking as I turned down my driveway. Remy left me feeling wild and unsettled inside. If Beck hadn't driven by, I had no idea how far that kiss could have gone.

There were kisses, and then there were kisses from Remy. Damn, this man kissed like no other. The way I felt when his tongue tangled with mine and his hard, muscled body pressed up against me was a mix of crazy, burning, yearning desire, and a deep, abiding wish to lose myself in him.

You see, Remy had gone and done the impossible. He made me forget. For good reason. He also made me *want*. I wasn't sure I would've wanted to stop at all. He made me forget how my confidence had eroded away inside and made me afraid to try anything when it came to men. With him, it felt so right, so effortless, and so easy.

I forgot every promise I made to myself about not letting myself feel vulnerable. Ever again.

That's why he was dangerous. Even more precarious, I felt as if he would protect me from anything. There was something about the strength he carried, like steel wrapped in velvet. Speaking of steel, I wasn't just talking about his cock.

I came to a stop in the little circular driveway in front of my house, hearing Henry's quick yip from the front door as I stepped out of my car. I loved coming home to a dog. Nobody, not even me, could show up at my house without Henry announcing it.

I took a shaky breath, trying and utterly failing at ordering my pulse to slow down and the flutters to stop spinning in my belly. The butterflies completely ignored me.

I wanted to rush away, not even to say good night. That wouldn't be polite though. Remy had changed my tire *and* made sure I got home safe. I would never say it aloud, but it meant the world to me to have someone make sure I was okay.

Remy was already stepping out of his truck before I could formulate a plan. I had to plan everything when it came to men. I couldn't seem to think when it came to him though. I hadn't been this rattled by desire before. Ever.

When I turned to look at him as he approached, with the soft glow of the light cast from my front porch, my breath caught in my throat. All of a sudden, I was awash in an old memory. Fear scattered through me, leaving me feeling numb and shaky in nothing more than a few seconds.

I was so relieved Remy was here. Scrambling for purchase in my mind, I tried to focus on him. He was tall and strong, and strangely, I didn't feel the least bit intimidated by him.

I didn't know what he saw in my face, but in two quick strides, he was in front of me, peering down, those rich green eyes skimming over my face. "What is it? Come on, sweetheart. You look like you saw a ghost."

Get it together, Rachel. It's just Remy. You're safe. Safe, safe, safe...

The word echoed in my mind.

I knew—at the very core of myself—I was perfectly safe

with Remy. I didn't know how I knew, but I did with such certainty, I didn't overthink it. That meant everything. That's why he was so treacherous for my sanity. I couldn't count on anyone to take care of me, other than myself.

But I couldn't quite be reasonable, not right now. Memory works in strange ways sometimes. It comes at you, flashing out of nowhere, at the strangest times. Called into consciousness by a scent, a time of day, a color, a sound. Or, in this case, a man walking toward me. Once the flash of fear hit me, it dissipated rapidly. Because I felt completely safe. It was so startling, I didn't know what to think.

Remy took another step closer. My pulse was in an out-and-out revolt against my mind, entirely oppositional and ignoring my attempts to slow it down. My belly clenched and my breath caught in my throat as I looked up at him.

I wanted him to kiss me. My desire was confusing on the heels of my jumbled flashback of fear.

"What is it, sweetheart?"

The low timbre of his voice tugged at my heart and sent a hot shiver skating over the surface of my skin. I swallowed and took a shaky breath, rattled for different reasons.

"I'm fine," I managed to say, my voice coming out raspy. I felt off-balance, my confused emotions, the past and all of its ghosts colliding in this moment, and not making any sense.

Henry let out a sharp bark, and Remy's lips curled into a smile, promptly sending my belly into another series of flips. "Henry isn't going to let anyone sneak up on you, is he?"

He couldn't have known how much weight his question held and how important it was that Henry absolutely did not let anybody sneak up on me. My throat tightened with emotion—relief, the safety I felt with Remy here, and the regret for the mistakes of my past, all twining together.

"No, he won't," I said as I turned away quickly, uncomfortable with how I felt inside. As I took a step, my foot caught on the edge of one of the slate flagstones marking the path to the steps that led to my front door. Remy steadied me, his hand catching one of mine.

He said nothing, and I marveled at the sense of comfort I felt with him. Although I hadn't spent too much time with him before, our social circles bumped in the small-town world of Willow Brook. I knew him to be quiet and always a gentleman. I'd heard a few women giggle about how damn handsome he was, and about his sexy southern drawl.

It would be difficult not to notice how ridiculously delicious and sexy Remy was. The potency of Remy was obvious simply from being in proximity to him.

Yet, now that I had a little taste of him, now that I'd gotten a little closer than I'd ever imagined I'd let myself get to a man again, it wasn't just his looks and his voice that were so damn tempting. Rather, it was the way I felt with him, contained in his strength, held within the circle of his protectiveness.

Oh, and more turned on than I had *ever* been in my life.

I stopped at my door once I cleared the steps onto the small deck at my house, my keys held tight in my grip. Thank God, because I was in such a fog of need since that crazy kiss, I probably wouldn't have known what I did with them.

Turning the key in the lock, I glanced back to him. "Thank you for seeing me home and for changing my tire."

"I've got your tire in the back of my truck. I'll repair it tomorrow," he replied.

Somehow, well, I knew exactly how—I was so damn flustered after that kiss by the side of the road, I hadn't even asked him what he'd done with my flat tire.

"You don't..." I began, my words trailing off when he shook his head.

"I'll take care of it, sweetheart. Give me your number, and I'll call you when I have it ready tomorrow."

He had his phone out, and I recited my number, watching while he tapped it into his phone. I didn't seem to know how to resist anything when it came to Remy. Not kisses, not fixing my tire, not anything.

I felt my own phone buzz in my pocket.

"I texted you. That way you have my number," he said with a wink.

I simply stared at him, nodding along. He dipped his head, brushing his lips across mine quickly. It was a brief kiss, nothing like the hot, crazy kiss a few minutes ago. Yet, the feel of his lips sent a spiral of heat through me, spinning straight to my core. My lips were tingling as he drew back.

"Good night, Rachel."

I heard myself say good night, the sound of Henry on the other side of the door nudging me out of my stupor. After I closed the door behind me, I listened to Remy's footsteps making their way down the stairs.

I fell asleep with him burrowing into my thoughts.

Chapter Six

RACHEL

"Hey, I need a favor," Charlie said, poking her head around my office door.

I looked up at one of my closest friends. "Anything. What's up?"

I worked at Willow Brook Family Medicine as a medical assistant, and Charlie was one of the doctors at the clinic. Charlie had her dark hair pulled back in a ponytail, with a few streaks of purple showing. Charlie's daughter, Emily, enjoyed dying it, and Charlie let her do whatever she wanted.

I tapped save on the note I'd just finished entering into a patient's chart. Along with this job, I did backup work at the local hospital. I'd started out here before Charlie moved to town, working for Dr. Johnson, or Doc, as most everyone in town called him. He recruited Charlie because he was getting up there in years and needed the help.

"I just got an emergency call over at the hospital. I'd love it if you could pick Em up at school and give her a ride over to the station. She's working this afternoon, and she'll be miserable if she can't go," Charlie explained.

"Of course. I just finished up. What time does the bell ring again?"

"Three. She'll be waiting outside. I'll text her and let her know you'll be there. Thanks a million," Charlie said. "I gotta run, okay?"

"No problem," I called as she hurried away.

I only had ten minutes to get over to the high school on time, so I took care of a few more things and took off. In short order, I was pulling up in front of Willow Brook High School. Emily was standing outside, waiting exactly where she needed to be. This wasn't the first time I'd done backup taxi duty for Charlie. I never minded. In fact, I loved it. Em was a blast. Like most teenagers, she was easier-going with me than she was with her mom.

She waved. Her short dark hair was tipped all over the ends with pink that glinted in the afternoon sunshine. She tossed her backpack in the backseat as she climbed in, glancing over as she adjusted her glasses on her nose.

"Hey, you get car duty today, huh?"

"Sure did." I waited to move as another car rolled past us to pick up another waiting teen. "All right. You've got ten minutes to get me up to speed on everything that happened since last week. What's up with Aaron?" I asked, referring to her boyfriend.

"Oh, nothing new. I'm trying to decide if I should have sex," Em replied casually.

I slammed on my brakes when we approached the stop sign. "No!"

Em burst into giggles. "Kidding. Calm down. I told Charlie I wasn't planning on having sex. She still made me get birth control though. I guess that's a good thing, right?"

"Ab-so-freakin-lutely. You're just messing with me, right?" I countered, worried she really was trying to decide if she should have sex.

"Of course. Charlie is way less freaky than you, and she

was all-business about the birth control," Em said with a
shrug.

"Because she's a doctor, and she knows how easy it is to
get pregnant," I said wryly, as I turned onto Main Street in
downtown Willow Brook.

Em called Charlie by her name because Charlie was both
her aunt and her mother. Em's mother, also Charlie's sister,
had died from cancer a few years ago. Charlie had adopted
Em with her sister's blessing before she passed away.

"You mean, she's more mellow about you having sex than
I am?"

"Of course she is. She's all practical about it. She told me
she'd rather me be honest with her and let her know, so she
gave me a bunch of condoms and made me start birth
control. I told her I could do one or the other and she said
no. That safe sex wasn't just not getting pregnant. I'm pretty
sure Aaron is a virgin too, though, so I don't think it's
happening anytime soon."

I was busy trying not to have my brain explode. Em was a
sweet, wayward teen with an attitude. I didn't even like
thinking about her having sex. I silently sighed. Of course, I
couldn't get all judgy. I lost my virginity in high school. But I
looked at Em, and I didn't want her to have sex, even though
it was none of my goddamn business really. I decided a
change of subject was in order. I knew Charlie had had the
straight sex talk with Em because she'd told me. "All right,
what else is going on with you and Aaron and whatever?"

"Everything's fine with me and Aaron. Nothing really
exciting. I'm all about being boring. We don't even sneak
cigarettes anymore. I'm not sure what's worse, smoking or
sex."

"Both," I said firmly.

Em rolled her eyes as I turned into the drive, slowly
approaching the far end of the parking lot at Willow Brook
Fire & Rescue. Em had ended up with a job here after Jesse,
Charlie's new husband who happened to be a hotshot fire-

fighter, had set up Em's community service here, after she got caught smoking under the bleachers at school last year.

Em adored her job and worked here three days after school. I couldn't help it when my pulse lunged at the sight of Remy's truck. I'd given Em plenty of rides here and never thought much about who was here when I dropped her off.

Remy had texted me today to let me know he had repaired my tire. Before I left to pick up Em, I had texted him back to tell him I would be stopping by the station. He hadn't replied yet, so I wondered if he was out and about.

When I climbed out of the car after Em, she looked over with a question in her eyes. "Oh, I had a flat tire last night, and Remy was driving by. He helped me change it. I guess he fixed my flat today too," I explained.

"Oh cool. Remy's awesome," she replied as she snagged her backpack and slung it over her shoulder.

Just the thought of seeing Remy had my body humming. He had planted himself in my thoughts. I must've replayed that kiss last night a few too many times already. I followed Em into the station, and she waved over her shoulder as she hurried down the hall toward the front. "Thanks for the ride. I'm due over on the police side today."

I blew her a kiss. "See you tomorrow afternoon." Tomorrow was Friday, when Em worked a few hours at the clinic and helped with filing.

I was about halfway down the hall, intending to go up to the front to check with Maisie and see if Remy happened to be around. At that second, the man in question stepped out, flinging a towel over one shoulder. My mouth went dry and heat bloomed from my core throughout my entire body.

Remy did not have a shirt on and his skin glistened with moisture. I presumed he had just taken a shower.

Oh. My. God.

The man was a work of art. His chest and his abs were muscled and cut. He wore a pair of jeans hanging low on his hips, drawing my eyes down to the V muscles that narrowed and disappeared behind the waistband.

Sweet Jesus. I *so* desperately wanted to see more.

"Hey, sweetheart."

Remy's husky drawl snapped me out of my greedy visual exploration of his body.

Whipping my gaze back to his face, I felt my cheeks heat. He didn't say a word, but I *knew* he knew I'd just been looking. I wasn't about to apologize. Remy had to know he was obscenely handsome. He'd been living in Willow Brook long enough for me to know that many women would be happy to use his body as a playground. It was all I could do not to reach out and touch him.

With him simply standing there, shirtless in front of me and his green gaze holding mine, my sex clenched, and I felt the slick heat building between my thighs.

In contrast to Remy's glory, I was wearing my usual work outfit. I was quite practical and usually wore scrubs. Today's pair happened to be hot pink with a little bunny on the shoulder. This particular pair was actually a gift from Em. She had declared her mother's choice of scrubs too boring, along with mine, so she had gotten each of us a variety pack of brightly-colored and decorated scrubs.

My hair was up in a messy ponytail, and I'd had a busy day at work. I also forgot my contacts this morning, so I adjusted my glasses on my nose, feeling self-conscious and frumpy.

Remy was quiet, holding my gaze for a beat before his eyes dropped down and then meandered their way back up. My nipples practically stood up and waved at him.

By the time his eyes met mine again, I didn't feel frumpy. Not one little bit. The heat contained in his gaze strummed a chord inside of my body. I had completely forgotten why I was there.

"Um, I was just dropping Em off. Charlie had to go to the hospital for an emergency," I finally said.

Remy nodded, cocking his head to the side. "I got your text."

"Oh! Wait, you have my tire."

Oh my God. I sound like a total flake.

Why, oh why, did I need to make it obvious I spaced out? Maybe someday I would learn to keep my thoughts to myself, but clearly, today was not that day.

Remy's slow grin did funny things to my insides, and I was suddenly worried I'd melt right here in front of him. "Hang on, let me grab a shirt. Your tire's out back."

I actually had to bite my tongue to keep from telling him not to put on his shirt. In fact, I was thinking it would be quite all right if Remy never wore a shirt. Ever.

Chapter Seven

RACHEL

I might've had skid marks on my tongue, but I managed to keep my mouth shut. He turned away quickly, stepping through a doorway immediately to his side. I didn't know how much time passed, but it wasn't much when he returned with a black T-shirt covering his glorious chest and a jacket hooked over his fingers. His blond hair was damp, his green eyes standing out with his skin slightly flushed.

Do not think about Remy naked in the shower.

My mind was clearly feeling oppositional and went straight there, sending a jolt of heat through me. I could feel the potency of his presence. He smelled fresh and clean, and I wanted to bury my nose in his chest and breathe him in. I also wanted to kiss him. Fiercely.

I was silent as we walked down the hallway, restless with a jumble of feelings spinning inside me. I knew what I wanted. Remy.

I honestly hadn't thought I would ever experience desire again. It was such a shock, it threw me off and sliced through my defenses.

I had plenty of reasons, all of them quite good, for

steering clear of relationships. I should've been having a little chat with myself about now, reminding myself why this was crazy. I was trying, yet there was another voice, a rather loud, opinionated one that I didn't quite trust.

Trust your gut. You know you feel safe with Remy. He's not like Bruce. You can't be alone forever. Well, I guess you can, but not for this reason. That's just depressing.

We passed through the back area of the station where there was a kitchen and a large hangout area with a television on the wall, clearly dedicated to video games as evidenced by the four guys sitting around bantering about some game. Another television was dark with a guy napping on the couch nearby. Beyond that was a glass encased workout room where several other guys were working out.

I'd been in here before, seeing as I was friends with a number of the firefighters. I tested myself, letting myself stare through the glass where a few perfectly honed, physically fit specimens were lifting weights. My test failed. Completely. My body didn't even feel anything staring at those guys. I could objectively appreciate their raw, masculine beauty, but nothing more. No *zing*, no electricity, no naughty heat sliding through my veins.

I tried to tell myself maybe something had finally switched back on in my body and that was why I was so drawn to Remy. If that were the case though, I should've felt a twinge of *something* staring at the other hot as hell guys working out.

Nothing, I felt nothing. Cutting my gaze to the side, I watched as Remy called out a teasing reply to something someone said. Hell if I knew what. It was safe to say I wasn't too focused.

The chiseled lines of his face and his full lips with his teasing grin were delicious and sent need spinning through my veins.

In another moment, we were outside, the cool air a relief against my heated skin. I was flushed inside and out and needed a cold shower to cool me down. The crisp spring air would have to do for now.

Even though I'd forgotten about my tire once I saw Remy, I'd had enough sense to park beside his truck when I arrived. Remy stopped at the back of his truck, lifting the cover and pulling the tire out with one arm. I thoroughly enjoyed the sight of his arm flexing. I never really noticed arms much before, but Remy's were sinewy and corded with a dusting of dark blonde hair against his bronzed skin.

My mind spun to how it felt to be held by those arms last night. Heat streaked through me again, and I had to order my body to behave.

"Want me to swap the tires out for you?" he asked.

My brain felt sluggish, hazed by his mere presence.

After too long of a pause, I forced myself to speak. "You don't have to, I'm sure I..." My words trailed off as a grin flashed across his face. "What?"

"Well, you didn't know how to change a tire last night, so I'm not guessing you're an expert yet. Let me take care of it. I won't feel right otherwise."

Well, how's a girl supposed to resist that?

He switched my tires in a matter of minutes. He brushed his knees off as he stood, hooking my spare tire in a hand and going to the back of my SUV. He had my tire put away before I could make a peep.

"Have dinner with me."

His voice slid over me like honey. God, I could listen to him talk all day. About anything. I was nodding before I even realized it. Sweet hell.

His lips kicked up at one corner, and my nipples tightened. When I looked up at him with a flush heating my cheeks again, all I could think of was the way his lips felt against mine.

"Yes?" His tone held the barest hint of a question.

You can't say yes. That new voice, a rather bold one, had a quick retort. *Hell yes, I can.*

"Yes," I said, the word coming out breathy and making me think I must sound ridiculous.

I cleared my throat as we stood there in the parking lot. Afternoon sunlight angled across the trees just beyond the parking lot. I took a deep breath, catching a hint of spruce and the earthy scents of the ground beginning to melt.

And Remy. Dear God, the scent of him was like a drug—subtle, but rich and musky, conveying the same potency he carried within him with such ease.

"Tomorrow then."

Something about how confident he was finally kicked my typically snappy self into gear. "Do you normally just tell women when things are going to happen?"

Remy's grin widened as he lifted his shoulder in an easy shrug. "No. You tell me when. I figured tomorrow was logical because it's Friday."

I wanted to argue the point, but somehow, I sensed that would be giving him what he expected. "Tomorrow is perfect," I said, lifting my chin. "Where should I meet you?"

"I'll pick you up, sweetheart."

I cocked my head to the side, finally feeling on my footing again. "Really? I can drive, you know."

"I'm quite aware that you can drive, Rachel. I followed you home last night." His slow, sexy drawl never failed to send heat skittering under the surface of my skin. "Please let me pick you up," he cajoled.

Once again, I couldn't resist and simply nodded. I expected that to be the end of it, but he surprised me, dipping his head and brushing his lips across mine. That brief contact sizzled across my lips, sending a spin of electricity through my system. I instantly wanted to feel his tongue tangling with mine.

There was something so delicious, so decadent, about kissing Remy. As desperately as my body wanted all of him tangled up with me, I also didn't want to miss a single second of a kiss with him. Remy was a man who savored, who called to the need inside of me.

He pulled back far too soon, after no more than a second. With a wink, he turned away. "Tomorrow. Six o'clock. You decide where." Then, he was holding my door open for me. Because he was that kind of man.

"You're bossy," I said, just before he closed the door.

All I got from that was a little chuckle, which only amped up the need gathering in my core.

Chapter Eight

REMY

Six o'clock. That was when I told Rachel I'd be there. I
didn't like to be late, but I was. We had an afternoon call,
nothing major, a car accident on the outskirts of the highway. As a hotshot firefighter during fire season, which was
mostly spring into autumn, most of my work took place out
of town. But now, when everything was damp from the
winter melt, the three crews based out of Willow Brook
rotated handling local calls.

Aside from the fact I had needed a change of scenery
down to my bones, the schedule was one of the things that
had drawn me to this position. I liked variety. Many hotshot
crews were only on duty for part of every year. Seeing as my
initial training had been straight-up firefighter work, I could
comfortably manage both types of work, not to mention
that I did *not* enjoy time on my hands.

I had texted Rachel to let her know I was running a little
behind and why. I'd hesitated to send the text, wondering if
she would use this as an excuse to put me off. But my mama
had raised me with manners. Since I knew I was going to be
late, I needed to let Rachel know.

Blessedly, she had simply replied with, *No worries, see you when you get here.*

Freshly showered, in jeans and a navy blue T-shirt, I turned down her road, anticipation already humming in my body. Ever since I kissed her the other night, she had crowded my thoughts in every spare moment.

Kissing her was like diving into heaven. Hot damn, she was lush and soft, and so responsive, I'd have happily taken her right there on the side of the road in the darkness.

It would've been quick, dirty, and pure heaven.

But there was more. Rachel poked and prodded at places I'd thought long off-limits. In fact, I'd shut them off on purpose. I didn't want to care. I didn't want anyone to be that important. Just my sister, Shay. She held a slice of my heart and always would.

Not that my feelings for Rachel were sisterly in any way. Hell no. It was just that Rachel tugged at my heart. When I dropped her off at her house the other night, there'd been a moment when I saw something flash in her eyes. Her vulnerability flickered, and all I wanted to do was shelter her close to me and keep her safe.

I was probably damn crazy. I was hypersensitive to worrying about women. For starters, my parents had been a bit old-fashioned.

My father had been a gentleman in the truest sense of the word. He raised me to honor women, to treat them with respect, and *always* take care of them. My mama had been sassy, strong, and opinionated, and he loved her to pieces.

So, there was that. Then, there was what happened to my sister. Shay had gotten tangled up with the wrong man, a man who almost killed her. If he wasn't behind bars for a damn long time, well, I couldn't say what I would do.

Somehow, Rachel slipped like smoke through the cracks of my defenses and curled around my heart. I wanted her fiercely, and I knew she wanted me. I wasn't going to walk away from this, even though part of me was terrified by it.

I knew far too well what it was like to lose someone you loved. I'd lost my parents so abruptly, I promised myself I would never let anyone matter that much again. Yet, I found I couldn't turn away from Rachel.

She met me at the door, looking so damn gorgeous, it was all I could do not to step inside, close the door, and tell her we should forget the dinner date and just get right to it.

Her glossy dark hair hung loose around her shoulders, straight and silky. Her blue eyes were bright, so rich and deep, I wanted to dive into them and learn all her secrets.

She wore a soft cotton skirt that hugged her hips and flared around her ankles. Her skirt was paired with practical leather boots and a loose white blouse. The collar dipped down, teasing and taunting me with the shadowed valley between her breasts.

Forcing my eyes back up to her face, my gaze snagged on her lips, plump and inviting. We'd yet to say a word. She swiped her tongue across her bottom lip, and that did it.

I closed the distance between us in one step, lifting a hand and sliding my fingers into her hair. Dipping my head, I brushed my lips across hers because I couldn't *not* kiss her.

The subtle friction sent a hot sizzle through me. At the sound of her breath catching in her throat, I swept my tongue into the warm sweetness of her mouth.

Rachel's hand slid up around my neck, teasing my hair. She seemed quite all right with my greeting, her tongue slicking against mine and a low moan escaping her throat. She smelled so damn good. The scent of her spun around me, hazing my thoughts and making me forget any manners I'd ever had.

Suddenly, there was the feel of a furry body wiggling against my legs. Henry, her dog that I met last week when she was covered in mud, nudged me out of the hot trance I was tumbling into. I drew back, a low chuckle slipping from my lips.

"Hello," I belatedly said, my voice gruff.

Rachel smiled, her cheeks flushing a pretty shade of pink and sending a shot of blood straight to my cock. She had the unique ability to make me feel like a randy teenager who had absolutely no self-control.

"Hi," she said softly, the husky sound of her voice spinning into the center of my chest and gripping my heart like a vise.

There was definitely lust when it came to Rachel, but it was all tangled up in an unfamiliar intimacy, a need to protect.

Henry gave a soft woof, and I stepped back, leaning down to pet him. "Hey buddy, you're a lot cleaner tonight," I said as I slipped my fingers through his fur. He was a gorgeous dog, black with gold markings with his fur silky soft.

He greeted me with his tail thumping against the backs of my legs. Straightening, I caught Rachel's eyes. "He's a good boy."

Her smile widened, and she leaned down to stroke him across his back. "He is. Are you ready?"

"Whenever you are," I replied.

She turned, leaning over to pick up her purse from a small table just inside the doorway. "Let's go then." Stepping through the door, she paused, her hand on the doorknob. "Be back, Henry."

Henry trotted across the living room to jump up on a chair. With his eyes on the door, he rested his head on his paws as Rachel closed the door behind her.

I didn't really think about it, but I caught her hand in mine as we walked across the porch and down the steps to my truck. It felt easy, and I couldn't bear having her close without touching her.

My body was running on high idle, anticipation revving inside. I had to have a little chat with my cock, ordering it to stand down. Much as I'd have been happy to take her right here and now, that wasn't quite how I wanted it to play out.

Once she was situated in the passenger seat and I climbed in on the driver's side, electricity crackled through the air when I glanced over to her. In the light of the setting sun with dusk falling, her eyes were bright, and her lips swollen and pink from our kiss.

My heart gave a hard *thump*. I was so screwed.

Chapter Nine

RACHEL

Spinning my almost empty wine glass between my fingers, I looked across the table at Remy. I was flushed all over, my body humming ever since I opened the door tonight.

He was so damn handsome. His dark blond hair and deep green eyes paired with his bronzed skin, well, it was too much. He exuded virile masculinity. My eyes kept lingering on the way his faded T-shirt hugged his shoulders, and I couldn't help but remember his delicious chest when I'd seen him at the station yesterday afternoon. I wanted to lick him all over.

Even worse, he was so nice. And that southern drawl? Sweet hell, my panties were wet just from him talking. It had not helped matters, not one bit, that he greeted me by kissing me. My lips were still tingling, and it had been a good hour since we arrived here.

He was quite the gentleman, insisting on getting my door and pulling my chair out for me, even though we were only having dinner at Alpenglow Pizza. It wasn't exactly a fancy place. It was casual—a brick oven pizza place with an open kitchen to the back of the small restaurant, booths on one side and tables to the other. The restaurant had opened in the last year or so and had quickly become popular. Willow Brook had, by some stroke of bad luck, gone without a pizza place for about five years after the last one had closed.

The owners had renovated an old barn on the outskirts of downtown. The old stalls had been transformed into the kitchen in the back, and they'd opened up the rest of the space for seating. The wide plank hardwood floors were refinished, and there was seating at the counter surrounding the brick oven in the back. The place had a relaxed, warm feeling. Plenty of windows let ample light in, so the space was bright, even in the dark winter months.

The windows to one side where we were sitting offered a view of a meadow with Denali in the distance. The snow was gradually receding on the mountains as spring took hold. I had only absently noticed the view, unless I counted Remy as part of it. My eyes soaked him in greedily.

Over dinner, we had chatted about a few things—my family, how I ended up becoming a medical assistant, and what he thought of living in Alaska. There was a lull in our conversation when his mouth hitched up at the corner, and I realized I'd been staring.

I blurted out the first question that came to mind. "So, tell me about your family. Where do they live now?"

His gaze shuttered, and he took a sip from his beer. "My parents died. My younger sister and me are all that's left of our family." His words came out in a low, even tone, but I could see the pain in his eyes, and it tugged at my heart.

Although I didn't know him that well yet, I knew he was a good man. I also knew whatever had happened to his parents was painful.

"Oh, I'm so sorry, Remy." Without thinking, I reached across the table for his hand. His fingers curled into mine, the sorrow evident in his eyes.

"It never gets easy to say that." He paused, taking another swallow of beer before setting the empty bottle on the table. "They died when a tornado blew the vacation home where they were staying to bits."

"Remy, that's terrible. I'm so sorry," I repeated.

My words felt entirely inadequate. My family meant a lot to me, and I couldn't imagine both of my parents dying at once.

Remy was quiet for a few beats, his gaze flicking down when he lifted his empty beer bottle. He brought his eyes to mine again and shook his head. The sadness was still there, but he seemed to be controlling it carefully.

"Yeah, it sucks. I don't have much else to say about it. Sometimes, the worst part is just telling people."

"I can imagine. It's natural to ask questions about family."

He was still holding my hand and gave it a squeeze. I didn't want to let go, although it crossed my mind that now would be about the time to do that. Yet, I held fast. I wanted that point of contact, and it seemed he did as well.

"Is that why you moved away?" I heard myself asking, and then almost immediately wanted to take the question back.

He shrugged. "Partly. I was a firefighter in my hometown. I had already scheduled my hotshot training before they died. I wanted to travel, so that part wasn't because of my parents dying. But then they did, and it became an easy way for me to escape. My training was in Northern California. I stayed there for a while after I finished my training, and then Ward... You know Ward, right?" he asked, referencing a hotshot firefighter who had moved here from California and also happened to be married to a friend of mine.

Pausing, Remy looked to me, then continued after I nodded. "I trained in the same location where Ward did. He's how I heard about the position that opened up here. I took it because I wasn't ready to go home yet."

"Do you think you'll ever go home?"

Remy was quiet, spinning his empty beer bottle with his

fingers. "I don't know. It's pretty heavy. I had my reasons for wanting to leave before my parents died. My sister had moved away for college before and was living with her boyfriend. She just recently moved back to the area to stay with some family friends. I'm not sure how long she'll be there, but that's where she is now."

I could feel his grief echo in his words. "Do you miss her?"

Remy smiled. "Shay's a special one. She's doing okay. I worry, but then I always worry. She tells me I'm too bossy and that she can take care of herself. She's living with an old buddy of mine. He had an extra bedroom, and I might've twisted his arm. His sister lives there too, so it's a good spot for Shay."

"Shay, that's a pretty name."

"That it is. She's a spitfire, always getting in trouble. Drove me crazy when we were younger. I talk to her a few times a week. That's about all she'll put up with from me, so it's probably good I'm not there. She says I'm overbearing."

I squeezed his hand at the low rumble of his laugh. "What do you think of Willow Brook?"

"I like it. I really do. I don't like big cities, but I like being close enough to get to one. Anchorage is a hop, skip, and a jump away, so that's convenient. When I came here, I was looking for a change. I got that, but I love my crew. I'd never pretend it's like the South where I grew up, but small towns have a lot of similarities, no matter where they are. This one's not so crowded. And now, there's you."

When he said that, dragging out the word *you* with his eyes darkening, my heart spun in my chest and my pulse bolted. Dear God. This man could melt me with nothing more than his eyes. Heat spiraled through me, making me hot all over. I shifted my legs to ease the ache building between my thighs.

He squeezed my hand again. "Shall we go, sweetheart?"

Oh. My. God.

Every time he called me sweetheart, my heart did a little dance. My throat went dry at the look in his eyes. His thumb brushed across the back of my hand, the calloused surface sending streaks of fire over my skin. I swallowed and took a shaky breath, pointlessly attempting to get my pulse to slow down.

"I bet you call all the girls sweetheart," I managed to tease.

His lips kicked up at the corner with a grin as he shook his head. "Nah, darlin' is my go-to. Sweetheart is just for you."

Oh. My. God.

Butterflies took flight, spinning wildly in my belly. "Oh," was all I could manage to that.

"You never answered me, sweetheart."

The blank look on my face must have cued him into the fact that I had completely forgotten what he asked me. With a chuckle, he repeated his question. "Shall we go?"

I dredged up my usual attitude and narrowed my eyes. "Sure."

Suddenly, it occurred to me we had rather swiftly moved beyond the news he'd shared about his parents. I paused. "I don't mean..." My words trailed off when he shook his head.

"It's okay. It's nothing to dwell on. Trust me, I'd rather not. Now let's go."

He stood from the table, catching my hand in his. He tossed a generous tip on the table before we walked away. His hand never let go of mine, even when he stopped to pay at the register, and my offer to cover half of the bill earned me an amused glare.

It didn't even occur to me to contemplate the implications of how natural it felt for him to hold my hand. That was the thing with Remy. Everything seemed to just unfurl. By and large, I thought I had mostly gotten past the mess of my last relationship. It ended in a glorious disaster, but not before my self-esteem when it came to men had been shredded to pieces.

In most areas of my life, I was my usual self—nosy, perhaps a little bossy, and funny. Yet, I hadn't even attempted to date in over a year. I'd resigned myself to the reality that I wasn't even interested in dating. In fact, I was quite convinced that was for the best.

I could barely consider it consciously, but there was a part of me that savored Remy's presence, the natural protectiveness he exuded. Once again, he had my door open before I could even reach for the handle.

I glanced up once I was seated, his gaze piercing in the fading light of dusk. "You're quite the gentleman," I said with a wink.

His mouth curled into a grin. That little bit of teasing attitude I'd latched onto burned up in the searing flame that spun through me. I could handle this, perfectly fine, as long as we kept everything superficial. It was just that nothing about Remy felt superficial.

"I'm a southern boy at heart. Maybe a bit old-fashioned. My mama raised me that way. She might not be here to give me hell about it, but I'm not about to let her down. I imagine she'd find a way to give me hell from heaven if I did."

At that, he carefully closed the door before rounding the truck to climb into the driver's side.

Chapter Ten

RACHEL

The entire ride home, I gave myself a little pep talk. This was just dinner. I could handle dinner. This was good for me. It was good for me to try to push out of my comfort zone a little. And Remy was safe.

Safe, safe, safe. That word echoed through my mind. I was so busy telling myself I could handle this that I barely noticed the drive home and was almost startled when I realized he was turning down my driveway.

Glancing over, I studied his profile for a moment. His dark blond hair was a little shaggy. It was straight and glossy enough that it didn't look too messy though. It teased along the back of his neck, tempting me to run my fingers through it. His eyes flicked over to me, and my pulse took off again.

My gaze fell down to where his hand rested on the steering wheel, hanging loosely across it. His hands were strong and sexy. I knew the way they felt, and I desperately wanted to feel them all over me. My eyes tracked down over his forearms. Who knew forearms could be so damn sexy?

My eyes lingered on the corded muscles as he steered his truck down the driveway, then I forced myself to look out the window. My driveway wasn't too long. I lived a few minutes outside of downtown Willow Brook. I'd bought the house myself, right after I finished my medical assistant program. It was nothing huge, a small house on a few acres. By most standards, the lot might be considered big. By Alaskan standards, it was small. It was just enough that I had some privacy. My two closest neighbors were within earshot. I'd never even worried about that, but now it mattered.

When I moved into the home, one of those lots had been empty. After everything that went down with my ex, I'd been beyond relieved to have my neighbors build there. They were friendly and nosy, which worked out great. Before my ex turned my life upside down, I'd never once thought it would be good to have nosy neighbors.

I gave my head a shake. I didn't want to think about that. Remy rolled to a stop in front of my house, and the first thing I heard was Henry's welcoming bark. My house was a small, ranch style home. It was a perfect rectangle with cedar siding and a bright purple metal roof. The purple was what tipped me over to making the decision to buy the house. The owners had left a few things unfinished, but my father had promised to help me finish it, and he did within the first two months of me moving in.

When he cut the engine, Remy glanced over. "I'll walk you in."

The air inside the truck felt loaded—heavy with electricity snapping between us. This was my first date with someone in over a year. I didn't even like to think about my last date.

Uncertainty gripped me, but I nodded. As I moved to open my door, Remy was there. For a big man, he moved fast.

Somehow, despite all the anxiety spinning inside me, his presence was comforting. I climbed out, his hand steadying me as my feet hit the ground. That little point of contact zipped straight to my core, coiling into the need that had been simmering inside me all evening.

It was close to dark now, the sun having set during dinner. There were a few lingering streaks of red, gold, and orange above the mountains in the navy sky, which my property offered a distant view of above the trees out back. The jagged ridgeline was visible with the stars glittering above it and a crescent-shaped slice of the moon rising.

I took a steadying breath as we crested the stairs onto my deck, wondering what Remy expected. I knew what I wanted, but I didn't dare let myself think about it. I wanted to just lose myself in Remy. It was such a luxury to be with him, to feel the sense of ease somehow tangled up in the intense intimacy that had caught hold between us ever since he first kissed me.

My heart was pounding so hard I could hear the echo of it through every inch of my body. My low belly clenched, and those butterflies took flight again. I managed to get my keys out and then promptly dropped them. Not just once, but twice.

Remy scooped them up and slid the key in the lock himself. He was quiet though, and didn't tease. Glancing up as I turned the knob, I said, "Hang on, Henry will be flying out the door."

The moment I opened it, Henry did exactly as I warned and came racing out. He paused to spin around my legs and Remy's, leaping up to kiss my face as I leaned down to greet him. Remy chuckled, running his hand across Henry's back as Henry dashed into the yard to take care of business.

I simply stood there, my hand curled around the leather strap of my purse. When I looked up at Remy, my eyes snagged with his. I couldn't look away. He was no more than a foot away, his green gaze darkening.

Before I even registered what was happening, he lifted a hand, trailing his fingertip over my lips, his touch like fire. "I've been wanting to do that all night," he murmured.

A raven called from the trees, the sound barely punc-turing the haze of desire clouding my mind. "You have?" I heard myself asking, my voice all breathy.

Remy scrambled my thoughts and stole my senses when-ever he was close. His hand trailed across my cheek, slowly tucking a loose lock of hair behind my ear. Stepping closer, he bent low to brush his lips across mine.

He drew back slightly, and a disappointed moan escaped to lose the feel of his lips against mine.

"I like you, Rachel."

My heart gave a hard *thump*. As cynical and wary as I was, I liked Remy. A lot.

All this time, I thought no man could affect me again. I thought I'd said goodbye to desire because it wasn't worth the bother and the emotional mess.

With Remy here, desire and need contained in his gaze, I forgot to worry.

"I like you too," I said softly, thinking it sounded silly when it felt anything but.

Henry butted against my legs, dancing around our feet and bumping me with his head.

"Let me get Henry in. He likes a snack whenever I come home. Come on in," I said.

This temporary break sent my pulse into the stratos-phere, anxiety spinning into my desire. I couldn't believe I was letting any of this happen.

Knowing it would be weird if I suddenly shifted gears, I stepped back, gesturing for Remy to follow me inside. He was quiet as I dropped my purse on a table by the door and walked quickly into the kitchen to get one of Henry's favorite snack bones to toss to him.

Henry gobbled it up in a single bite. I laughed, catching Remy's eyes where he stood by the door.

The front entrance led to an open style living room. There was a small woodstove in the back corner, and windows along the back offered a view of the trees and the mountains. I'd situated my sectional couch so I had a view outside from one side with the other facing the television on the side wall.

The living room was separated from the kitchen by one side of the three-sided counter in the kitchen. Stools for seating ran along that side. The space was open and airy. I loved it, even though I had considered moving out last year. I still thought I would, I just had to catch the timing right.

A vivid memory flashed as my gaze scanned the room, snagging on a spot where Bruce had punched a hole in the wall. The hole was fully repaired, the sheet rock sanded meticulously one evening when I was determined to erase any visible reminders of what Bruce had done. Only I still knew *exactly* where the hole had been, but then, I knew exactly where every one had been. There had been five.

"You okay?" Remy asked.

It was uncanny how easily he tuned into me. I didn't know what to make of it. The kitchen was only steps away from the door. He took another stride, his eyes skimming over my face.

I took a shuddering breath, forcefully kicking those memories away. No matter what, I didn't want to let the past ruin the present. My eyes shifted to Henry as he trotted across the living room to curl up on his favorite chair.

Henry always made me smile, and right now he had the same effect. Looking back to Remy, I commented, "I'm fine."

I didn't know what pushed me to do what I did next, maybe my desperation not to let my past crowd into the present. I closed the distance between us and leaned up to kiss him.

Remy didn't miss a beat. As my lips brushed against his, a little sigh escaped, almost in relief. When he fit his mouth over mine, a thrill chased through me, straight to my core and radiating outward. On the heels of a low growl, he slid his hand into my hair. I gasped when his other hand slid down my spine to cup my bottom, and he pulled me flush against him.

His mouth slanted over mine, and our kiss became fierce. I couldn't get close enough, pouring all the emotion and desire pounding through me into the tangle of our tongues. Stroke for stroke, nip for nip, I lost myself in Remy.

His hand threaded in my hair, a subtle edge of roughness to his grip that I savored. Shifting my thighs, my hips bumped the kitchen counter. In a smooth motion, he lifted me up on the counter without ever breaking our kiss.

Given that I was about to melt into a puddle at his feet, it was a relief not to have to hold myself up anymore. Although I knew without question he was a strong man, there was something so encompassing about his strength. I felt held and protected, yet not overpowered.

His fingers sifted through my hair, his palm sliding down my spine in a heated pass. He gripped my hip, tugging me close to the edge of the counter as he stepped between my knees. My skirt had fallen in a rumple just above my knees.

I could feel the hard length of him pressing against me, the denim creating friction against the thin cotton of my panties. I barely recognized myself. I was gasping, low moans escaping here and there, and flexing into him as he drew back slowly and caught my bottom lip in his teeth with a gentle tug. His lips traveled along my jawline, teasing in my ear before he blazed a sizzling trail down my neck.

Fire gathered inside, and my nerves lit up, sending a prickly awareness whispering over my skin. Remy murmured something. I gasped when he cupped my breast, his thumb teasing back and forth over the tight bead.

"Remy," I gasped.

He lifted his head, his thumb still teasing me, and my nipple begging for more—tight and achy. "Yes, sweetheart?" he asked in that sexy southern drawl, yet another thing that nearly sent me over the edge.

I managed to drag my eyes open, only to find his gaze

waiting—dark, hooded, and so hot it seared me, a straight line to my sex. My panties were wet, and my hips were rocking reflexively against him.

With the full force of his intensity on me, I felt suddenly shy, almost overwhelmed at the mix of emotion and arousal coursing through me. I bit my lip and shrugged. "I don't know." He dragged his thumb across my nipple again. "I know that feels good," I murmured.

Without ever once looking away from me, he eased his grip on my hip, lifting his free hand and flicking the buttons at the top of my blouse open. Cool air hit my skin, the contrast only serving to notch up the heat burning me up inside.

"You're so fucking beautiful."

I swallowed, caught in a wave of emotion. Having largely shut myself off from men, I was unaccustomed to this kind of attention. Given my last relationship had been nothing but an exercise in emotional, psychological, and physical abuse, I was utterly undone at the look in his eyes and his words.

"Don't worry, we're not taking this too far tonight."

My brain interpreted that as if he were going to stop. I curled my legs around his hips. "Oh no, you don't get to go yet."

Remy's laugh sent a shiver over the surface of my skin. "Oh sweetheart, don't worry. I'm not going anywhere. Not just yet." He arched into me, the full length of his arousal pressing against my core and sending a sharp streak of pleasure through me. "I was about to ask if you wanted me to stop."

He paused, his gaze boring into me.

"For the record, the second you tell me to stop, I stop. It doesn't matter when that is."

I swallowed, again overcome with a wave of emotion. Remy had come out of nowhere in my life, the electric desire I felt with him utterly shocking me. It felt as if an asteroid had landed on the planet of me. Attention, respect, safety, and burning desire were not things that went together in my world. With him though, they did.

I nodded and then he flicked another button loose, dipping his head and dusting kisses along my collarbone and down into the valley between my breasts. My sex clenched at the feel of every kiss, each point of contact sizzling through me. Another button and then my blouse fell open.

He drew back slightly, a low growl escaping. "More beautiful than I imagined," he murmured, before dipping his head and sucking one of my aching nipples into the wet heat of his mouth, right through the silk of my bra. I cried out, the pleasure so acute, it pierced me.

After another hard suck, he transferred his attention over to my other breast. I buried my fingers in his hair and held on, clinging to my control and wondering if it was possible to have an orgasm from nothing more than this.

I felt the flick of his thumb on the clasp. My breasts tumbled free, and his calloused palm cupped a bare breast. I was murmuring his name and rocking into him, little bursts of pleasure striking every time I felt his arousal press against me.

His palm slid up my leg, sending shivers all through me and sparks skittering under the surface of my skin. He trailed his fingertips over the damp cotton between my thighs. All I knew was I wanted more.

He stilled, just long enough that I dragged my eyes open and finally let go of my death grip on his hair. "I want to make you come."

His blunt words pierced through me. So direct, so straightforward, and so fucking hot, I almost didn't know how to take it.

"Please do," I finally said, just as my hips telegraphed what I wanted with a rock against his palm. His mouth hitched at the corner, and he dipped his head again, trailing hot gentle kisses mingled with sharp nips along the side of my neck.

With one thumb brushing across my nipple, he teased over the wet cotton between my thighs. I was frantic for more. I wanted all of him. *Now.*

On a low growl, he shoved the fabric out of the way, sinking a finger into my channel. I paused and shuddered around him. I was so slippery wet, he slid in easily.

Another finger joined the first, and the subtle stretch felt so good, I almost came right then. He held still for a beat when I cried out before drawing his fingers back and teasing over my clit lightly. I was so close to the edge, chasing the sweet relief. His fingers sank inside again, fucking me with a few slow strokes. The moment his thumb teased over my clit again, it was like detonating a bomb inside my body.

Pleasure exploded through me, hitting me hard and fast, and then radiating through the rest of my body. The piercing sensation of my climax was so intense, I cried out as my body quivered in its aftermath.

Remy drew his fingers out slowly, his hand curling over my thigh as he pressed a kiss to the side of my neck. That kiss sent a little shock wave of pleasure through me.

As I slowly became aware, rising through the haze of sated pleasure, I opened my eyes to find him waiting. Sweet hell, he was so damn handsome. With his hair mussed, his lips a little red and swollen from our kisses, and desire still contained in his gaze, my heart gave an odd beat. The intensity of this moment almost overwhelmed me.

I shifted, reaching between us. I may not have had a relationship in a while, but I knew the expectations. I slid my hand over the rough denim, savoring the feel of his hard arousal under my palm. His breath hissed through his teeth, and he shook his head slowly.

"Not now, sweetheart. That was all for you."

Chapter Eleven

REMY

Rachel stared at me, her blue eyes wide, skin flushed, and her lips puffy from our kisses. Fuck me.

This woman.

It was taking about all of my control not to fuck her. Right here. Right now.

Quick and dirty.

I didn't even know why I was insisting on waiting. It was something about those glimpses of vulnerability in her eyes. There was also something about the way I felt when I was with her.

I didn't want to rush this. I hadn't had much sex lately. It was hit or miss. In fact, sex had become impersonal and brief. Nothing more than a means to an end.

I didn't want whatever this was with Rachel to be like that. I wanted, I craved, the slow build, the anticipation. I knew if I waited, it would only be that much hotter, that much sweeter, that much more intense, and that much more intimate.

With her blouse hanging open, and her glorious breasts bare for me, it was all I could do not to dip my head and catch one of her taut nipples in my teeth again. I wanted to give a hard suck before sheathing myself in her slick heat.

I shackled my need and clung to my control.

"All for me?" she asked, the husky sound of her voice catching little hooks in my heart, notching up the need inside that much more.

My cock was so damn hard, I knew I'd be taking care of matters at my own hand when I got home. I ignored my cock's protests.

I squeezed just above her knee. "That's right, sweetheart. All for you."

Something flickered in her eyes. Her hand stilled where she had it curled over my cock, and her gaze shuttered as she pulled her touch away. "Okay," she replied, her tone flat.

I didn't like that. I didn't think she was shutting me out consciously, but I sensed someone had done a number on her. She curled one hand tightly over the edge of the counter and worried her bottom lip with her teeth.

"Don't. I don't know what you're thinking, but if you think for a second that this has anything to do with me not wanting you, think again. I want you so bad, it hurts. But you're more than that. I want to make sure you know this is more than just one night."

Rachel's mouth fell open. "Oh."

"I'm on duty for the next few days. I'll text you, and we'll have dinner when I'm off."

I reached for her hand, pressing it over my arousal again. "*This* is all because of you."

Her eyes widened. When I leaned forward and caught her lips in a kiss, it was all I could do not to forget my promise to myself not to turn this into a quick, dirty fuck. When I drew back, her gaze was dark again and her lips curled into a slow smile.

"You're quite convincing," she said.

I grinned as I stepped back. "Three days."

———

The following morning, I rolled out of bed, my cock hard. I was alone and woke from a dream about Rachel. Although I had taken care of matters last night, it didn't seem to matter. I wasn't up for another lonely release, so I took a cold shower.

Women didn't usually grab hold of me the way Rachel did. I was a little frustrated that my crew happened to be on a three-day rotation. Thank God I loved my job.

Since I had moved to Willow Brook, I had bought a place close to town, no more than a five-minute drive from the station. Although I hadn't known how long I wanted to stay here, it seemed a smart move to buy rather than rent. My house was on a few acres with a pond off to one side, a small field on the other, and a mix of evergreens, cottonwood, and birch trees scattered around. The small two-story ranch was a timber frame home and blended into the surroundings. It had two bedrooms and a bathroom upstairs, and the downstairs was essentially one large open space, with the exception of another bathroom and laundry area. There was a soapstone fireplace to one side with the kitchen to the back.

After I showered, I headed downstairs, dragging on a pair of sweatpants and a T-shirt, the hardwood floor cool under my bare feet. The living room offered a view of the field out front with the sun striking the tops of the trees. I'd yet to see this home in the summer because I bought it last fall. For now, the front lawn was a bit muddy with a few patches of snow left in the trees.

I angled across the living room where there was a sectional couch and a few chairs with a coffee table. One of the draws to purchasing this home had been that it came fully furnished. The prior owners had moved out of state and rented it for a few years, leaving all the furnishings behind.

That made it an easy sell for me, aside from the fact that the price was right and I liked the property.

I started the coffee and then spun around, searching for my phone when I heard it buzzing somewhere. I spotted it on the corner of the counter where I must've tossed it last night when I got home. Striding over and glancing down, I saw my sister's name flashing on the screen. Lifting it, I slid my thumb across. "Hey Shay. What's up?"

"I haven't talked to you in a few days. Just calling to see how you're doing," she replied.

Shay and I spoke every few days, no matter what. For a while, I had called a bit more, but that was back when her asshole ex had been putting her through hell. He was in jail for years now, and that was more than fine with me.

"Well, I just rolled out of bed, and I'm waiting for coffee. What are you up to? You're four hours ahead there."

Alaska had its own time zone, an hour behind the Pacific time zone. With Shay back east, she was a full four hours ahead.

"I'm making coffee and about to go meet Jackson for a tour of the rescue area. I thought I'd call you while I'm waiting."

"You give him hell for being late, okay?" I teased.

Shay laughed. "Uh, no. Seeing as I just got here a few days ago, I won't be giving Jackson hell about anything. I'll leave that to you. I'm just glad Ash called me about staying here."

"It's going okay there?" I asked.

I was glad my best buddy and his little sister had a room for Shay at their family's farm, but she'd been reluctant when I suggested it. She didn't like anyone having much of an opinion about her life. She considered me—or anyone, for that matter—worrying about her, a nuisance.

I just wanted her to be somewhere where I knew she would be okay. She'd lost just about everything when things went to hell with her ex. She'd never married him, but he isolated her so thoroughly, she hadn't had anywhere to turn after our parents died. I'd almost left my job and gone back there, but she'd vehemently protested that.

"Of course it's going okay," Shay replied with a sigh. "You don't need to keep worrying. I'm fine. Clint is long gone. I know I screwed up, but nothing like that is ever going to happen again. As far as I'm concerned, I don't plan to date. Ever again."

"Shay, nobody, absolutely nobody, judges you for what happened, so stop saying you screwed up."

She was quiet for a moment and then another sigh filtered through the phone line. "I know you don't, but it doesn't change the fact that I blame myself."

"Shay..." I began.

She cut me off. "I'm figuring it out, Remy. I'll get through to the other side, but just let me find my own way."

The only time I questioned my choice to move so far away was when it came to my sister. Before I could say anything else, she continued, "And don't you dare feel bad for being in Alaska. It was the best thing for you after what happened. As much as I love you, I don't need you hovering over me. You know you would, so don't lie," she finished with a little laugh.

I smiled at her laugh, but my heart ached a bit. I hated what Shay went through, but I also knew her well. She was a fighter. She'd always been headstrong and willful when we were growing up. After the fiasco with her ex, well, that was the only time she let me step in and help her. I didn't know if I would ever stop wondering if I was too late. There was still so much I didn't know about what happened before she ended up in the hospital.

I shook those thoughts away, focusing on the moment. "I know, sis. You've told me forever that I didn't need to be bossing you around. I guess I'm glad Jackson is there to do it for me."

She snorted. "Right, because I love that. Anyway, tell me what's new with you. Please tell me you found a girl."

Shay was as protective of me as I was of her. After our parents died, my girlfriend at the time had broken up with me. Not right away, but a few months later, saying I was distant and emotionally unavailable.

She'd been quite right. I was barely tuned into life, much less romance. Cheryl and I, well, we'd been comfortable enough. I suppose my parents' death had illuminated some of the gaps in our relationship. Namely that we'd stayed together mostly because it was comfortable.

Although Shay had been disgusted with Cheryl, I completely understood why she broke things off. It had hardly registered for me. Since then, Shay had left me in peace about my personal life, until about six months ago. Out of nowhere, at least as far as I could tell, she decided it was time for me to fall in love.

That was a good reason not to be living in the same town as her. I could only imagine her matchmaking attempts if I lived anywhere nearby. She couldn't see me smile, but I did. "I can't say I've fallen in love, but I did take someone out to dinner last night."

The fact that slipped out surprised me. Shay squealed so loudly I had to pull the phone away. "Turn down the volume," I said when I put the phone back to my ear. "It was just dinner."

On the surface, that was true. Yet, Rachel was something else. She poked and prodded at my heart. My cock had a pretty strong opinion about what I should have done last night. Dinner was *not* enough.

"I don't care if it's just dinner. The fact that you took anyone out is amazing. Tell me all about her."

I laughed, shaking my head. "Her name is Rachel, she has a dog named Henry, and she's beautiful."

"I don't care what she looks like, Remy. Does she have a good heart?"

Shay was about as sentimental as it was possible to be. I thought of the look in Rachel's eyes when we were close, and my heart squeezed. Although there was a lot I didn't know about her, I knew without a doubt that her heart was true.

"Yes, Shay, she has a good heart. It was just dinner."

"Promise me you'll give her a chance," Shay said, her tone softening.

Shay had shared her opinion with me, quite a few times, that she thought I was shutting myself out from loving anyone else. She was quite right, but I wasn't about to admit it. Not out loud.

The way Rachel made me feel was unsettling, yet the force of her was too powerful for me to ignore. I didn't know what was going to happen, but I wasn't going to walk away without letting it play out.

"I promise, Shay."

When do you see her again?"

"What is this? Twenty questions?"

"Do I get twenty questions?"

I threw my head back with a laugh, glancing over when the coffee maker beeped, indicating the coffee was ready. Phone in hand, I strode over and snagged a mug out of the cabinet above as I spoke. "No, I'd rather not give you twenty whole questions. I'm on duty for the next three days, but I told her I'd call when I'm off. Good enough?"

She squealed again. "Yes!"

"All right, I gotta go. I need time for a shower before I head into the station. Tell Jackson I said hello. Okay?"

"Of course. Love you, Remy."

"Ditto."

Chapter Twelve

REMY

Late that afternoon, I set the chainsaw down, pulling my leather gloves off and sinking down to sit on a fallen tree. Ward tossed me a bottle of water from where he sat a few feet away.

"Thanks, man," I said with a nod before unscrewing the cap and almost completely draining the small bottle.

With it being spring, there weren't many fires to deal with, not just yet. We'd flown out to a nearby area, which had been hit hard by spruce bark beetle kill over the last two decades. We were taking the time to do some burn prevention and hopefully minimize fires if they got started, creating several channels through the wilderness to serve as firebreaks. Once things dried out a little, but before it was too dry, we would do a controlled burn. In the meantime, we were camping out here for three days. I actually loved this kind of work. It was hard and physical and kept me from thinking too much.

Leaning back on one of my hands, I glanced up toward the horizon. From this part of Alaska, Denali, the tallest peak in North America, was a centerpiece of the landscape. It towered in the distance.

Glancing to Ward, I said, "This is beautiful country, man."

He tossed me another water bottle. "That it is," he said, his mouth curling in a slow smile. "I love it here. How you like it so far?"

"Like I said, it's beautiful."

I didn't speak much about why I had moved here with my crew, but Ward knew. He knew because we trained together. He knew I had been delayed for my training because of my parents' death. One thing I liked about Ward as a superintendent, and as a friend, was he didn't push on issues. He let things lay low, but he was there if you needed him.

After I took another few gulps of water, I continued, "Willow Brook's a nice town. With Anchorage nearby, I can get my city fix. But I like things quiet, and Willow Brook is definitely quiet."

"Wait until summer," Ward said with a chuckle. "The population nearly triples, if not more. How's your sister?" His question felt almost like an afterthought, but I knew it wasn't. Ward paid attention to details, even if he didn't say much about them.

Shay had come out to visit while I was in California at my hotshot training, so Ward met her. "She's good."

A few other guys meandered over. We were finishing up for the day and needed time to set up camp. We weren't really roughing it where we happened to be right now. With a staging area set up, we had a big canvas tent where we could crash. In fire season, we were on the move. With the ground damp and no risk of fire, we had the rare pleasure of a campfire that evening.

The guys were teasing about a call last week. "You know Carrie. Now she's got *two* freakin' cats climbing trees. Is there going to come a point where we can tell her she can't get another cat?" Jesse Franklin asked.

Beck chuckled. "Nah. Stopping by to help Carrie is easy. I'll take that over the fucking call out to that asshole, Bruce Sutton. I'm just fucking glad I didn't have to deal with him."

"He's out of jail?" someone asked.

I idly listened, not thinking much of it.

Beck nodded, his gaze sobering and a hint of anger appearing. "Oh yeah. Did his time, and now he's out. He's already shacked up with some chick. He punched a hole in the wall, and she called the police, or so the report said. He was booked, posted bail, and went back on that same night. Thing that pisses me off is we already saw his game with Rachel, and I hate seeing it happen to another woman. It's a bunch of fucking bullshit. I don't understand why guys like that should even be able to date."

When I heard Rachel's name, my ears perked up. Ward shook his head slowly, rolling his eyes. "Totally agree with you on that. But, it's a free country. Don't think any law will keep him from dating. I hope he got charged with something."

Beck nodded. "Rex wasn't on duty, but one of his guys charged him, even when his girlfriend tried to back out of it later."

"Who the hell is Bruce?" My question surprised me. Normally, I'd keep my curiosity to myself.

Ward glanced my way. "He's an asshole."

Beck piped up. "He moved here a while back. You know Rachel, right?" At my nod, he continued. "She started dating him, and things got ugly. It was hard to see how that played out. She finally got out, and he faced some pretty serious charges by the time all was said and done. I was hoping when he got out of jail, he wouldn't try to come back here."

"You okay?" Ward asked. I didn't realize I was nearly crushing the plastic water bottle in my hand until I saw his eyes flick down.

I eased my grip. "I'm fine. Just hate hearing shit like that. My sister went through something similar. Her ex damn near tore her up. The damage on the outside is bad enough, but the rest is even worse."

"Your sister okay now?" Beck asked.

"Yeah, she is. Her ex was facing charges and then got himself in an even bigger mess with a DUI, where he ended up killing two people in an accident. He's in jail for a damn long time now between all the charges. So, yeah, I've seen more than I ever needed of assholes like that."

"Damn straight. I get it. Rachel's a good friend, and I don't even like thinking about him being in town," Jesse chimed in. "I'll have to let Charlie know. She sees Rachel every day at work, and they're tight, so she might want to have a heads-up Bruce is around."

"Any kinda restraining order in place?" Damn, my questions were just slipping out. I knew far more than I ever wanted to know about the way the legal system worked for women who ended up in these situations. It was slow and nothing but paper as far as I could tell. Court documents didn't keep anyone safe.

Jesse nodded. "Yeah, some kind of long-term one. According to Rex, those aren't easy to get."

"Yeah, but they're just a fucking piece of paper," Beck added.

Later that night, as I stretched out in my sleeping bag in the cool spring night, I knew the minute I was back within range of a computer, I'd be looking this guy up. I needed to know exactly what he looked like. It fucking tore me up to think someone hurt Rachel. It made me wonder about the shadows I'd seen passing through her eyes.

I fell asleep, thinking that the deep rush of protectiveness I felt for Rachel might be a bit too intense for the short time I'd known her.

Chapter Thirteen

RACHEL

My pulse pounded in a steady rhythm as my feet struck the ground. I dodged a rock and grinned as Henry paused ahead of me on the trail, his tail wagging madly.

Henry loved running with me. Well, I didn't know if it was running with me particularly. He loved any excuse to be outside. By chance, this was the first time I'd had the time and the weather cooperation for another run since my encounter with Remy. My glorious muddy fall, that is.

There was still plenty of mud, but I didn't mind, jumping over a puddle and continuing my pace. The air was cool, scented with the richness of spring. The sun's rays filtered through the trees, casting dappled patterns across the trail.

By the time Henry and I reached the end of the loop, I was sweaty, tired, and exhilarated. During the winter, I had to make do with an elliptical, so it was always refreshing to be able to get back outside.

I slowed near the trailhead, shifting to a walk and clipping Henry back on his lead. I preferred not to have him loose when we got to the parking area, just in case there

were any cars passing by on the road. The trailhead was on a
side road off the main highway leading into Willow Brook.

Henry nudged my knee when we reached my SUV. I
reached into the back to pull out his portable water bowl,
quickly filling it from the water jug I kept in the back. As he
lapped at the water, I glanced up at the sound of a vehicle
slowly turning into the parking area. When my eyes landed
on the driver, my heart stuttered to a stop, and I was frozen
with fear. My gut began churning, and I felt sick.

Bruce, the man who had haunted my dreams, shredded
my self-esteem, and made me wonder if I was plain stupid,
was driving. He rolled down his window and came to a stop
at the back of my vehicle, effectively blocking me in.

Before Bruce came into my life, I never would've even
noticed a detail like that. But I'd learned, painfully and
brutally, just how important it was to pay attention to every
little detail.

Bruce stared at me, his expression blank. His brown
hair was cropped close to his head, and his blue eyes were
bright. I couldn't believe I'd ever considered him handsome. My thoughts tumbled back to the last time I saw
him. It was at court when he accepted a plea deal for his
assault against me, the worst one yet. Up to that point, in
the short six months of our relationship, he'd been more
cunning and careful. He'd only left bruises on my arms, or
legs. Once on my stomach, when he punched me in the
side.

But that last time, he punched me in the jaw, leaving a
nasty bruise on the entire side of my face. I'd been fully
prepared to testify and had felt let down when they offered
him a plea deal. One year in jail, and a one-year protective
order once he was out. I was supposed to take comfort in
the fact he would stay on probation for three years due to
his history of assault before he'd ever assaulted me.

I was frozen inside for a few moments. Blessedly, cold
anger rushed in to fill the space opened up by my fear.

"Get the hell away from me," I finally said. Henry's hair rose on his back, a low growl coming from his throat.

"I'm not anywhere near you. Didn't even realize that was you," Bruce said, his tone low, the menace I knew so fucking well simmering under the surface.

He rolled the window up and drove away. I stood there, the fear rushing back the minute my anger was deflated. I moved stiffly, my hands picking up the water bowl and dumping what little water was left on the damp gravel.

Henry sensed my distress, keeping his eyes trained on Bruce's vehicle as it moved away, disappearing down the road. He stepped closer to me, his body warm against my leg. My knees were shaking, and I could hardly breathe.

After everything played out, I recalled asking a friend how in the hell I hadn't seen it coming. She pointed out the obvious. If abusive men started out showing their true colors, they'd never get the chance to hurt anyone. That had been cold comfort, although I had slowly come to understand I was one of millions and millions of women. Nothing more than a statistic.

In some ways, that was comforting. In others, it was so depressing if I let myself think about it too much. All I would do was cry.

I took a shuddering breath and let it out slowly. After Bruce was locked up, I just wanted to be alone. The joy of not living in fear was so pure it was startling. Even now, I was still shocked at how a mere six months in a single relationship had changed my life forever.

As soon as Bruce was in jail, I'd gone to the animal shelter and brought Henry home. Henry had become far more than a guard dog. He was my best friend. Just now, my usually wild dog held still and let me absorb his strength.

Several more minutes passed while my body vibrated with leftover fear before I glanced down to him. "You ready to go?" Henry licked my knee in reply, his tail thumping against my thighs.

Once Henry was settled in the back, I climbed into the driver's seat, instantly locking the doors. I'd gone from being hot and sweaty from my run to cold and clammy. So cold, I was shivering all the way through to my bones.

I cranked up the heat, wondering where the hell Bruce went. I contemplated whether I should report this to the police. No matter what Bruce said, I didn't believe him. I should've known he would come find me as soon as he got out of jail.

I was confused though, because I was supposed to receive a notification on the date of his release. I'd quite effectively quit counting the days, because I hadn't wanted to let that run my life. Before I drove away, I checked my phone calendar. His originally scheduled release date wasn't for another few weeks.

On autopilot, I drove into town. Without thinking, I found myself turning into the parking lot at Firehouse Café. It didn't surprise me. Whenever I was at loose ends, a few minutes with Janet James, the owner and an old family friend, usually settled my nerves. The town's original fire station, a stately, square building, had been transformed into a coffee shop and bakery years ago. The former garage offered seating for customers, with an open style bakery and kitchen in the back.

Pushing through the door, the familiar surroundings eased the tension knotted in my chest. Fireweed flowers wound around the old fire pole in the center of the space, the dashes of bright colors creating a warm, cheerful space. The tables to one side had scattered customers seated, and I breathed a sigh of relief when I saw Janet restocking the bakery display behind the counter.

Janet's brown eyes crinkled at the corners with her smile when she saw me. "Hey Rachel, what brings you here this time of day?"

Stopping in front of the counter, I curled my hands over

its smooth, rounded edge and opened my mouth, only to have nothing come out.

"You okay?" Janet asked in return, closing the sliding case door from the back and setting down the now-empty tray in her hands. Her dark hair was liberally streaked with silver and twisted into a braid. She brushed her braid off her shoulder as she regarded me, her eyes narrowing in concern.

I sighed. "Not really. I just ran into Bruce. I didn't know he was in town."

I didn't need to explain further because Janet knew the whole, awful, embarrassing story. She rounded the counter, looping her hand through my elbow and tugging me into the back. Once we were out of sight of customer, she pulled me into a hug. Janet was warm and round and maybe the best hugger in the universe. She squeezed me hard and then stepped back.

"You go right to the police station and talk to Rex," she said firmly.

"Maybe I'm overreacting..."

Janet shook her head. "Absolutely not. If you don't talk to him, I will."

Looking into her kind gaze, I managed to take a deep breath finally. "Okay."

The sound of the bell above the door out front jingling reached us. "You need to get back to work," I said when Janet just stood there, one hand still resting on my shoulder.

"It'll wait. You want some coffee? Something to eat?"

I chewed on the inside of my cheek and smiled softly. "No, I'm all set. Just needed a few minutes. You get to work."

Janet hesitated until I nudged her shoulder. "Come on. I promise I'll go talk to Rex now."

Minutes later, I pulled up in front of Willow Brook Fire & Rescue. I sat in my car for a moment, wondering again if I was overreacting. I'd yet to determine what the worst part of ending up in an abusive relationship was. The constant self-doubt and questioning was probably the most pervasive. It invaded every corner of my life, leading me to doubt even basic, no-consequence decisions sometimes. Just now, I kept questioning whether it was just by chance Bruce had been driving by, and worrying I was being dramatic.

My gut told me otherwise, quite insistently.

Henry's friendly face loomed behind me in my rearview mirror—black with gold markings and such earnest eyes. Reaching back, I stroked his head, and he licked my hand. My shaking had finally stopped, and I took a slow, steady breath.

Just now, it occurred to me this was the day Remy had said he would text me. I'd done my best not to be too nosy, but it was quite convenient that Charlie happened to be married to Jesse, another hotshot firefighter. I could glean bits of information about the crew schedules from her without even asking.

In passing, I heard from her that Remy's crew was scheduled out for three days doing some clearing in a fire prone area. Remy was conveniently on the same crew as Jesse. I wondered if they were back yet and if I would see him.

Remy had been filling my thoughts for days—he'd given me one of the most intense orgasms I'd ever had in my life. The yearning to be closer to him nearly swamped me whenever I thought about him.

Layering into that was the sense of safety I experienced when I was with him. Right about now, I wanted to search him out and burrow into him. Emotion lodged in my throat. I hated what had happened with Bruce. It was so embarrassing, and I wished I could hide it from Remy.

In the small town of Willow Brook, which I loved most of the time, I wouldn't be able to keep that ugly part of my past a secret. Especially not with Bruce back in town. Another wave of emotion hit me, and I swallowed through the tightness in my throat.

Don't fucking cry over him. He's already caused you enough pain.

On the heels of another shuddering breath, Henry stuck his head between the seats and pressed against my shoulder. Just as I was wondering if I could simply back out and drive away, the door to the front of the building opened and Maisie Steele waved at me.

She probably saw my car. I rolled the windows down a bit for Henry, gathering every ounce of my courage around me, and climbed out.

"Hey," I called.

"Saw you pull up," she replied. "What's up?"

I reached her side and tried to force a smile, but I wanted to cry.

"Hey, what's wrong?" she asked, her arm sliding around my shoulders as she turned and walked us both through the door.

I was relieved there was no one else out in the front area. Just a few empty chairs, and Maisie's "control station," as she liked to call it. Maisie was a good friend and ran the dispatch line here. Dispatch in Willow Brook was essentially gossip central and Maisie knew everything. She happened to be on duty the night I finally called the police on Bruce last year.

She kept her arm around my shoulders, pausing beside the counter that circled her desk. Her wide brown eyes were concerned as she peered at me. "What's wrong?" she repeated.

A side bonus to the fact I could be a bossy bitch was, when necessary, I could kick myself through moments like this. I gave my head a shake. "Fucking Bruce is out of jail," I spit out, latching onto the anger swirling inside.

Her eyes widened further. "What?"

"The stupid phone warning system didn't let me know. I checked my calendar and his original release day wasn't for another few weeks. Maybe I'm being ridiculous, but I decided to let Rex know that he showed up where I like to go running with Henry."

Maisie shook her head, her wild brown curls bouncing along with the motion. "I'm guessing he got an early release due to overcrowding—which is bullshit, if you ask me—or for good behavior. I can't leave the front, but you go talk to Rex right now," she said, tugging lightly on my shoulder and aiming me in the direction of the door that led to the police side of the station.

"You sure you don't think I'm overreacting?" I asked.

"Hell no," Maisie said firmly, just as the station phone buzzed.

"I have to get that since I'm on duty. Go talk to Rex," she said, hurrying around her desk. "Nine-one-one, what's your emergency?"

Her question rang behind me as I pushed through the door into a small hallway. Rex Masters was the chief of police for Willow Brook and had been for years. His son, Cade, was one of the superintendents for the hotshot fire-fighters. I was close to Cade, and to Rex's daughter, Ella, since we went to high school together. Rex was a bit like family, which had made it all the harder when I ended up in that clusterfuck of a relationship with Bruce.

On the list of things life didn't prepare me for was how I would feel when I stumbled into that disaster. I considered myself a strong, smart, independent woman, but inside of a matter of months, I was afraid to tell anyone what was going on and I had no idea how to get out of the situation in which I'd found myself.

In hindsight, God-awful as it was that Bruce got so violent that night, it was a blessing. It had pushed me over the edge to call for help.

Chapter Fourteen

RACHEL

I knocked lightly on Rex's open office door. Rex looked up, cracking a smile.

"Rachel," he said, waving for me to come in. His hair was more salt than pepper these days. His weathered face and ready smile were reassuring. No matter what, Rex gave off a comforting air, as if he would personally make sure it would be okay.

For a beat, I considered leaving the door open, but I didn't want anyone to walk in on our conversation. I closed it behind me and slipped into one of the chairs across from his desk. He removed the glasses perched on his nose. Rubbing his eyes, he smiled again, glancing down at his glasses.

"I told Georgie I didn't need these. She laughed at me, so I had to admit she was right. Anyway, I meant to call you today."

"Bruce is out."

Just saying his name aloud sent a burst of fear through me. I pushed back against it, harnessing my anger.

Rex sighed. "Like I said, I meant to call today. I was out of town until this morning, but I got back and saw the report that Bruce was booked for another assault. I didn't even know he was out of jail, much less that he was in town. Got a call in to the jail, but my guess is he was released sometime in the last few weeks. I don't think he landed in Willow Brook any sooner than last week. Someone would have seen him."

"I have the long-term restraining order. I saw him today. He showed up at the trailhead where I like to run when the weather's good. I don't know if I'm overreacting, but I'm pretty sure he knew I was there. He tried to play it off and said it was just an accident." My stomach churned. "How did I not know? I was supposed to be signed up for that stupid alert system."

Rex nodded. "The guy covering for me while I was out didn't know the background. They booked him, but he bailed out the same night. I'm sorry, Rachel. If I had known ahead of time, I definitely would've let you know. It was just chance this happened while I was out of town."

I wanted to cry and scream all at once. I'd been constantly beating back that fear for the entire year since Bruce had been in jail. The six months I'd spent with him loomed so fucking large in my life. I hated it. It had changed everything, including me. I never guessed I could stumble into a train wreck like that.

Still clinging to my anger, I held Rex's gaze. "I don't know why the hell he came back to Willow Brook. Can you charge him for violating the restraining order?"

"I'll damn sure try. The D.A. has to clear it, but I'll do my best. Tell me exactly what happened," he said. He spun in his chair, shifting his laptop on its rotating tray in front of him. "I'll enter the report right now and call it in to the D.A. before you leave."

I told Rex exactly what happened. He was helpful, but not certain. "Either way, this gives me an excuse to go have a little chat with Bruce. If the D.A. agrees to press charges, obviously we will. If not, it will be because he claims he just saw you by chance. I'll explain to him that if he pushes it, he *will* face charges."

Rex glanced down at his laptop and back to me. "Look, guys like him keep trying—again and again. When I heard about the charges when I got back today, I hoped it meant he moved on from you. Based on his track record before you two tangled, he's not used to women kicking him out of their lives that fast. Don't take that to mean I'm glad he's knocking somebody else around. I just hate to see him pull this crap with you."

I took a shallow breath, realizing my fingernails were digging into my palm. I released my grip, flexing my fingers. "Do I know her?"

Rex shook his head. "Don't think so."

I chewed on the corner of my lip, letting out a slow sigh.

"Let me call the D.A. right now, okay?"

At my nod, Rex picked up the phone. He quickly summarized my report, nodding along to whatever the D.A. said on the other end before he hung up.

"I'm not surprised, but she thinks we need to let this one slide. It warrants a conversation. This way, when it happens again, we can explain we gave him a chance to understand the ramifications. I'm gonna go track him down right now," Rex said as he rose from his chair.

As we exited his office, he glanced back. "I know you like to take care of things yourself, so thanks for stopping by. We're going to nip this in the bud."

At that, he waved and headed down the hallway toward the back of the station. I returned to the front, waving to Maisie because she was tied up on the phone. She immediately lifted a hand, gesturing me over to her desk.

Just as I reached her, she ended the call and pulled her headset off. "Hey, how'd it go?"

"Rex is going to go talk with Bruce. I can't believe it, but he was arrested a few days ago."

Maisie sighed and nodded. "I just figured that out. The call came in the night I was off. I've emailed the whole damn station to tell them they are to let me know if any call comes in about Bruce, even if I'm not on duty."

"That's not..." I began.

Her curls bounced when she shook her head. "I can't believe this slipped past me. You don't get to tell me what to do, so deal with it. I just called Beck and gave him hell. They just landed today, and he said he heard about it while they were out."

Maisie's protectiveness made me want to cry. I had good friends and that was a blessing.

"It's been over a year since his arrest," I finally said. "I'm sure I would've found out soon enough. Not that I really want to know. I just want him to get the hell out of town."

The door to the back swung open, and Beck, Maisie's husband, came walking through. "I didn't know until this weekend, and we were in the middle of nowhere," he said immediately, his gaze swinging between Maisie and me.

"I'm fine, Beck. It is what it is," I replied.

Beck leaned his elbow against the desk. "It still sucks. Trust me, the entire police force and all the guys are up to speed now. If any calls come in on him, we'll know."

Maisie flashed him a smile as Beck rounded the desk to drop a kiss on her cheek. Before Maisie moved here, I'd have been surprised to see Beck settle down. He was downright domestic now. He adored Maisie, and they had two toddlers already.

As Beck straightened, the door from the back opened again. This time, Remy came walking out. I was an emotional mess inside. The burn of adrenaline was still pumping through my body, and the anger I'd latched onto to keep me from falling into a mess of tears was still running hot.

In the middle of that mess, the sight of Remy was a jolt through my body. His dark blond hair was like burnished gold, his green eyes bright as they coasted over my face. He looked surprised to see me. Meanwhile, I wanted to fling myself in his arms and forget everything else.

Chapter Fifteen

REMY

Rachel stood by the counter in front of the station. Even though we had an audience, I couldn't keep my eyes off her. She was so fucking sexy and beautiful. Her glossy hair was pulled into a ponytail, her cheeks were flushed, and her eyes bright. She wore a T-shirt over fitted fleece leggings.

I presumed she'd just been running. When I studied her eyes for a moment, I knew she'd been crying. A mix of anger and vulnerability was contained in her gaze with a hint of desire flashing in the depths as we stared at each other.

Beck's voice snapped through the weighted silence between us. "Well, I'm gonna head out back. When's your shift over?" he asked, glancing to Maisie.

When I looked in their direction, Maisie's curious gaze was bouncing between Rachel and me. Belatedly, she looked over at Beck. "In a half hour. Are you going to wait for me, or head home? Max and Carol are at your mom's."

Now, Beck was delayed in responding, with a knowing glance between Rachel and me. It was clear both of them had picked up on something between us. He swung his eyes back to Maisie. "I'll go pick them up and meet you at home. Okay?"

At her nod, he leaned down and caught her lips in a quick, but fierce kiss. That man was so damn whipped, it was almost ridiculous. He was forever being teased by the guys around the station, and he didn't give a damn. Allegedly, he'd once been a bit of a player, but I found that hard to believe. Beck adored Maisie and was all-in when it came to being a father. I never once even heard him complain about having two toddlers around the house.

Straightening, he threw a smile at Rachel and me. "See you around," he offered with a wave before pushing through the door into the back. Conveniently, the dispatch line buzzed. Maisie quickly answered, shifting into work mode.

Rachel stepped a few feet away from the desk. "I was just stopping by. I..."

Her words trailed off, and I filled the silence. "I was about to text you. Dinner tonight?"

Her eyes widened with a small smile, her cheeks pinkening. Damn. I wanted to kiss her, something fierce.

"Um, okay. Where do you want to go?"

"Just tell me where, and I'll pick you up."

The truth was, I didn't give a damn what we did. All I wanted was a few hours with Rachel. Actually, I wanted more than that, but I'd take whatever she'd give me.

Yet, I sensed something was unsettling her, and I wanted to know what it was.

"If you don't mind, I'm not really up for going out. I'll cook you dinner. Henry loves visitors too," she added.

"Tell me when."

Her gaze flicked to the clock above the door in front of the station. "Six o'clock?"

"I'll be there."

Just then, a truck pulled up out front. Rachel turned her head to look out the windows. She visibly flinched then stood frozen, staring out the window.

What the fuck?

The truck came to an abrupt stop, jerking forward and back. The man driving slammed it into park. Just as he climbed out, Rex came wheeling into the parking lot, his lights flashing as he came to a quick stop behind the truck, boxing it in.

The man in question turned to face Rex as he exited his patrol car, raising his hand, his middle finger extended. I couldn't say how I knew, but I knew Rachel's reaction was to this specific man. I didn't even think and turned to her, curling my hand around hers. "Come on, let's go in the back."

A fine tremor was running through her body, and I wanted to pull her into my arms. Even though I was blind to the details, my gut told me that man outside had hurt her.

As I turned to the back, I caught Maisie's eyes. She mouthed, "Thank you."

I was relieved Rachel simply went with me. She didn't say a word as I held the door open and walked her down the hallway. About halfway down, Beck stepped out of his office, gesturing for us to go in. I guessed Maisie must have texted him.

As soon as the door was closed, Rachel sank into a chair by a small round table and buried her face in her hands. The sound of her ragged breathing was audible in the room. I was flying a bit blind here, so I sat down in a chair at an angle across from her.

"You okay?"

She was quiet for a minute before she lifted her head, her eyes glittering with tears. "I'm fine. Fucking fine!" Her anger was fierce, a force in the room. "That asshole out front represents the biggest mistake of my life. I know we barely know each other..." She paused when I shook my head.

I answered the question in her eyes. "Not barely. Before last week, I considered you a friend, even if I didn't know you that well. But now I know how you feel. Don't pretend I don't know," I said, my words coming out stronger than I intended.

Rachel opened and closed her mouth, her cheeks flushing. "Okay. My point was you didn't know that I ended up in a disaster. That asshole out front"—pausing, she gestured toward the front of the station—"beat the shit out of me, and now he's out of jail."

Fury slashed through me, but I beat it back. I didn't know what Rachel needed right now. "You obviously made sure he got the hell out of your life," I said, my voice low.

It killed me to see the pain mingling with the anger in her gaze. I wanted to wrap her in my arms. I wanted to make love to her, and I wanted to wipe that asshole off the face of the earth. These conflicting impulses tangled up inside me in a storm of emotion.

"I'll kick his ass for you." Considering we were at the police station, I wasn't going to be getting away with punching that asshole, not right now, but it didn't change the fact I'd be happy to do it for Rachel.

A bitter smile crossed her face, and she shook her head slowly. "Nah. He doesn't even deserve that much energy. Will you do me a favor?"

"Anything."

"I don't want to leave until he's gone, but I don't want to walk out to see if his truck is still there. Can you check?"

Reaching over to tap the speaker button, I called Maisie's inside line. She was going to see it as a call from Beck's office, but that probably worked in my favor.

Proving me right, she answered quickly. "What's up? We have a situation—"

I cut in. "It's Remy."

"Oh, sorry, didn't mean to be rude. I thought you were Beck."

"I figured as much. Just letting you know I'm back here in his office with Rachel. I've got you on speaker. Can you let us know when that asshole is gone?"

"Oh, thank God. Are you okay, Rachel?"

Rachel sighed. "I'm fine."

"All right. Well, Rex is talking to him. As soon as they're gone, I'll tell you. Oh, wait. He's already getting in his truck."

———

A few hours later, I turned into Rachel's driveway. I was still mulling over the events at the station. After Maisie reported Bruce was leaving, I went out front to confirm he was actually gone. Rex had assured Rachel if Bruce showed up anywhere near her again, he would arrest him, and the D.A. would press charges.

I hadn't wanted Rachel to leave alone, but her expression had turned downright mutinous when I suggested I follow her home. I had to bite my damn tongue and resist the urge to follow her against her wishes. The moment she left, I practically stormed into Rex's office to get the background.

Rex had hesitated to fill me in until he took a long look at me. "Well, I guess I don't have to worry too much."

I hadn't cared to debate his implications.

I heard Henry's bark through the door as I climbed the steps to her house, and was damn relieved she had him. I knew he wouldn't let anybody show up here without raising a ruckus. After I heard her telling Henry to be quiet, the door swung open. Her hair was down, hanging loosely around her shoulders, the glossy brown tempting me to thread my hand in her hair and kiss her, right here and now.

It was more than her hair that made me want to kiss her. Her lips were so fucking tempting with that plump bottom lip and the slow curl of her smile when she looked up at me.

"Hey, come on in. Henry's going to go nuts if he doesn't get to say hi."

Oh right. Henry. I loved dogs, but greeting Henry wasn't as high on my priority list as kissing Rachel was.

But I grinned and stepped through as she shut the door behind me. Kneeling down, I let Henry circle me with wags, his tail thumping against my back as I stroked his head. "Hey buddy," I said before straightening. He trotted across the room, picking up a multicolored rope toy that he sent flying in the air and caught as it fell.

Rachel laughed. "Henry entertains himself. Come on over," she said, gesturing to the kitchen as she walked toward it. Her hair was damp, and I presumed she had showered since her run. I was slightly disappointed she wasn't still wearing her fitted T-shirt and leggings.

Not that I had any complaints about what she was wearing now. She'd changed out of her running clothes into a stretchy cotton skirt with a long sleeve T-shirt. Her breasts pulled the cotton tight and curved over the top of the V collar. Her feet were bare and her toenails were painted bright purple. Something about the whimsical color made me smile.

She pointed to one of the stools beside the counter. "Have a seat, I'm just finishing up. Do you want beer or wine, or something else?"

"I'll take a beer."

Opening the refrigerator, she glanced back over her shoulder. "You have choices," she said before reeling off three different options.

"I'll take the darkest of whatever you have," I replied.

A moment later, she handed me an open bottle of beer and turned to check something on the stove, adjusting the heat on the burner.

Hooking my feet around the legs of the stool and taking a drag from my beer, I asked, "Do you like to cook?"

"Oh, I love it. I'll never be one of those people who can be thin and diet because I like food too much."

"Whatever you do, don't change a thing," I murmured, thinking it would be a damn shame for Rachel to try to do anything to lose her gorgeous curves. Her cheeks flushed pink when she looked back at me.

A while later, after Rachel practically shooed me out of the kitchen when she started cleaning up, I took Henry out for a bathroom break with her permission. After I returned inside, he trotted over to the chair in the corner, leapt onto it, and almost instantly fell asleep. Rachel closed the dishwasher and turned to face me, her hands curling over the handle.

This evening had been a test, a test I never thought I'd have to pass. Our encounter this afternoon and hearing about Bruce had me torn up inside. I was swamped with the urge to protect Rachel. Yet, I sensed she might not appreciate that.

My internal tug-of-war over the strong pull I felt toward her was largely pointless. My intellect took a backseat to the rest—the desire knotting me up inside and keeping me on edge ever since I'd seen her this afternoon, the unfamiliar possessiveness, the need to claim her.

I saw Rachel's eyes flick to the door behind me and guessed she was checking to see if I'd locked it when I came in with Henry. I knew that habit from Shay. It was something I never thought much about, ever in my life. Hell, I never even wondered about doors being locked when I was home. I didn't worry about it for me, but I knew it mattered to Rachel.

I reached behind me and locked it. Rachel's eyes slid back to mine, widening. She opened her mouth as if to say something and then snapped it shut.

"Do you want to talk about what happened this afternoon?" As soon as I asked the question, I wanted to snatch it back.

We didn't need to weigh in to that heavy topic. Rachel stared at me and I wished I knew what she was thinking. Her eyes shuttered, and her cheeks flushed deeper. After a moment, she shook her head.

"There's not much else to say. I hate that it's a part of my past, but it is. There are a lot of things you can change, but the past isn't one of them."

She uncurled her hands from the handle on the dishwasher, crossing the kitchen to where I stood at the edge of the counter. I was a muddle inside—concern and desire spinning together.

Eyeing me, she rested a hand on her hip. "Whatever you think, don't you dare feel sorry for me," she said, her tone low and controlled. "I got through it, and I will get through whatever bullshit he throws my way again. Don't feel bad for me about what happened. It was my own damn fault, and I should've seen it coming."

None of this made me feel sorry for Rachel. Protective? Possessive? Angry as fucking hell with the asshole who did this? Yes, yes, and yes. Absolutely.

"It didn't even cross my mind to feel sorry for you," I said, closing the distance between us. "But don't you dare fucking say you should have seen that coming. My sister went through something like that. It has nothing to do with seeing something like that coming. When you have a good heart, you expect the same from others. I know you're strong and smart. That's the problem with assholes. They expect people to give them the benefit of the doubt. We do."

She stared at me, her eyes flashing. After a moment, a flicker of sadness crossed her face. "I'm sorry about your sister."

"You're breaking your own rule. Don't be sorry. She's good now. Like you, she got out, and she's okay."

Rachel laughed softly. "You're right." She looked at me for another long moment and then lifted her hand, tracing it along my jawline. "I don't want to think about that anymore. It's the past, and that's where it's going to stay."

She took another step closer, her soft curves bumping against me. My breath hissed through my teeth when she curled her hand around my neck and leaned up as she pulled me down for a kiss.

Chapter Sixteen

RACHEL

I was a jumble of need, emotion, and yearning. After this afternoon, I toyed with texting Remy and calling tonight off completely. My emotions felt volatile, too close to the surface, pressing against my skin. The anger had faded, leaving me feeling exposed. I hated how vulnerable I felt when I thought about Bruce.

Yet, the urge to see Remy was so powerful, every ounce of common sense I had couldn't beat it back. I wanted to lose myself in the wildness between us. The not-thinking part of me wanted to burn my regret, frustration, and pain to ashes in the force of the fiery desire between us.

I was under no illusions. I didn't think Remy was going to save me. I didn't think I'd ever have the kind of happily-ever-after you hoped for once upon a time before life sent you skidding into a tailspin. No, I considered myself lucky just to have one night with a guy who wasn't an asshole.

This thing with Remy was like lightning striking dry grass. You couldn't catch it. If you tried, it would singe you. The only choice was to let it strike and burn free.

As mortified as I'd been to have Remy see me at a weak

moment, the mortification fed into my frustration and anger, and spun into a resolve of steel inside. Bruce had once shredded me to pieces inside. I finally got out of that situation, but I was stronger now, and I wasn't going to be ashamed of my past. I'd been afraid Remy learning about Bruce would chase him away, but that didn't seem to be the case.

When I slipped my hand up around his neck, my fingers teasing his shaggy hair, I breathed a sigh of relief when he didn't hesitate. Bending low, he fit his mouth over mine—a brush of his lips, a soft nip, and then his tongue swept inside when I arched into him.

Dear God. Remy kissed like a god—a mix of soft and gentle, rough and hard, and the contrast sent me spiraling inside.

One of his hands cupped my cheek, his thumb brushing across the crest of my cheekbone, before sliding it into my hair and gripping lightly. The subtle sting on my scalp was welcome. Every sensation he elicited was laced with pleasure.

His other hand slid down my back, the heat and strength of it so delicious I moaned into our kiss. The sound seemed to spur him on. Cupping my bottom, he rocked his hips into the apex of my thighs. The feel of his hard arousal through the rough denim of his jeans elicited a gasp.

Everything was sensitized—my skin tingled all over and slick heat built in my core. I'd been wet pretty much since Remy showed up tonight. He was so fucking sexy. He had a straight line to my desire, his presence all that was necessary to amp me up.

With his tongue stroking against mine, I mapped my hands over his chest, savoring the hard planes and the contrast to my softness. He muttered something roughly when my nails scored his back through his T-shirt.

Breaking free from our kiss, he murmured, "I don't know how far you want us to go."

Although he hadn't framed it as a question, I knew he was asking one. Sweet hell. This man was going to slay me—body, heart, and soul.

Although Bruce had left scars, he never had a shot at my heart. Remy was close to stealing it already.

"Oh, we're not stopping," I said, holding his gaze.

If this was the only night I allowed myself this decadent pleasure, there wasn't a chance in hell I was letting it pass me by.

When Remy's mouth curled into a slow smile, sending my belly into flips and my heart thudding hard and fast, I practically fell over.

"Good thing we're on the same page. In that case, where's your bedroom, sweetheart?"

One word, just a casual endearment, and I almost melted.

Taking a shallow breath, I stepped back, catching his hand as I turned. Glancing over to check on Henry, I saw him deep in sleep in his favorite chair in the corner. I'd never brought a man home since I'd had him. Usually, he slept at the foot of my bed. I didn't particularly mind if he did that, but I didn't want an up close and personal audience, not right now.

As I led Remy into my bedroom, I was beyond relieved I had gotten rid of every piece of furniture after Bruce came through my life like a wrecking ball. This was the modern world, and it wasn't like I thought everything had to be fresh. But all of that held memories I didn't want. Getting rid of everything connected to him had been cleansing.

Stepping through the door into my bedroom, I nudged my elbow on the light switch, the two lamps in the corners flicking on low. At the sound of the door clicking shut behind us, I had a moment of intense anxiety. Before Bruce, I'd been reasonably confident when it came to sex. But in a matter of months, Bruce had ruined sex for me. He was perpetually unsatisfied and always blamed it on me. I knew now—far too late to stop what happened—that was a common issue with men like him.

The effect was so destructive that Remy was the first man I had kissed in over a year.

I beat back the sense of anxiety. For a moment, I was afraid I was going to freeze up. Wordlessly, Remy took care of that instantly. His hands slid down my sides where I had stepped into the room ahead of him. There was something about his touch, so strong and so sure, bordering on worshipful.

"Turn around, sweetheart," he murmured, the gruff sound of his voice like a hot caress.

It was impossible not to do what Remy asked. Maybe that was a me thing, but I couldn't imagine any woman saying no to him.

Turning, I collided with his liquid hot gaze. Remy was all man—unapologetic, virile masculinity. And the way he looked at me—it's a miracle I didn't simply melt like butter.

"What?" I asked when he stayed quiet.

His gaze heated as his eyes dipped down to travel over my body and back up. "Oh, I'm just wondering how fast I can get all those clothes off."

I swallowed as heat flashed through me. The chemistry between us was so powerful, it overrode all the doubts crowding for space in my mind. The doubts that usually had me thinking too hard, wondering if I was doing the right thing, or the wrong thing. With Remy, it was all sensation driven by pure desire. It was such a relief not to think.

I laughed and then shimmied out of my skirt, flinging my T-shirt to the floor with one hand. This time, when his gaze swept up and down my body, I could feel the burn of it on my skin.

With an ache building between my thighs, I shifted my legs restlessly. Remy was right there in front of me, his lips dusting hot kisses over my shoulder, his hands, so big and rough, sliding over the curves of my hips. His hardness such a contrast to my softness.

"Sweetheart, you're just about gonna kill me."

I swallowed, meaning to say something. Whatever it was dissolved into a breathy sigh as he lifted me easily, striding a few steps to my bed before stretching me out over it. He straightened and reached behind his neck to pull his shirt off in one motion.

I'd gotten a glimpse of his chest that afternoon at the fire station but somehow, I'd forgotten the glory. My mouth went dry, my sex clenching as he flung his shirt to the side where it joined my clothes on the floor. While I was busy absorbing the sight of him, he kicked his boots and jeans off and stood before me in nothing but a pair of briefs.

His arousal was quite evident. I was acutely aware of the wet silk between my thighs. The thought of him filling me had my sex clenching.

Before I had time to formulate anything remotely resembling a thought, Remy was stretching out beside me on the bed and pressing kisses in the valley between my breasts. My hands were greedy, mapping his chest, sliding down over his hard ass and rocking into him when he rolled partially over me.

I wanted everything. All at once. But my want was quickly supplanted by the sheer torture he put me through. Pleasure and need collided as he explored me with his hands and mouth, sending sparks scattering through me.

The entire world narrowed to this—Remy and me, tangled up together. He kissed me everywhere it seemed. I was restless, my hips rocking into him almost frantically. Meanwhile, he took his sweet time, leisurely making his way down my body, mapping kisses across my breasts and belly.

One of his palms teased along the inside of my thigh as he pushed my knees apart, settling his broad shoulders between my thighs. Restless, I rocked my hips into his touch as he trailed his fingers over the wet silk. He rolled to the side, hooking his fingers over the edge of my panties and dragging them off so efficiently I barely even noticed.

"Damn, sweetheart. All for me," he murmured, the rough satisfaction in his words sending a wash of heat through me.

He dragged a fingertip through my slick folds, eliciting little gasps and pants from me. I needed more.

"More?"

I must've said that out loud. Two thick fingers sank inside just as he put his mouth against me. I almost came instantly when his tongue swirled around my clit and he drove his fingers deeply inside. Remy made me crazy, so sensitized just by being near him, I was already at the edge.

Dear God, the man's tongue was talented. He drove me wild with lazy swirls over my clit, as if he had all the time in the world. He fucked me slowly with his fingers, pushing me closer and closer to the delicious edge.

I was gripping the sheets as I gasped his name, a broken chant, begging and pleading. With another deep drive of his fingers, he sucked my clit into his mouth. Pleasure burst through me, shattering me, and leaving me ragged and boneless.

I felt him draw away, instantly missing his closeness. Opening my eyes, I saw him produce a condom from somewhere. For a flash, I worried if he would even fit. Remy was a large man. He easily cleared six feet by several inches, with a heavy muscled body to match, and a long, thick cock to go along with the whole package.

I barely had time to absorb the sight of him before he rolled the condom on, his rich green gaze pinned to me in the dim light. "Now's the time to tell me if you don't want things to go any further," he said, his words gruff and intent.

Ever since he sent me flying the other night, I'd been trying to tell myself this was just sex—way overdue, hot, and delicious sex.

While that was quite true, the way I felt when I was with Remy was something more—something electric, that caught on the edges of my heart and strummed through my body, a chord vibrating only for him.

"Don't you dare stop," I heard myself saying.

His lips curled at the corner, one of his deliciously sexy half-grins. With his eyes locked to mine, his knee pressed down between my thighs, the mattress dipping as be brought his weight down over me.

I was discovering that Remy didn't do anything quickly. His hands slid slowly up my thighs and sides as his hips came to rest in the cradle of mine. The calloused surface of his palms sent sparks of heat across the surface of my skin as he cupped my breasts, briefly brushing his thumbs across my tight, achy nipples.

Then, he was dipping his head, dusting kisses along my collarbone and up my neck before he found my mouth. His tongue slipped in, nice and slow, as I moaned his name into our kiss.

When he rocked his hips against me, the hard length of him slid through my slick folds. I was soaked from need and the juices of my last climax, so wet my thighs were damp.

It didn't matter that I'd found my release only moments ago. All I wanted was *more*.

Too soon, he drew away from the wet heat of our kiss, and I whimpered.

"I need to see you, sweetheart," he murmured.

My eyelids were heavy, but I managed to open them, looking into his hot gaze. He rocked his hips again, the underside of his cock sliding over my swollen clit. Pleasure spun through me, eddies of my last climax—sharp, piercing, and sweet.

"Remy," I gasped, my voice ragged and needy, his name nothing more than a plea.

"Right here, sweetheart." With a subtle shift of his hips, I felt the thick head of his cock at my entrance, my legs shifting reflexively to make room.

He slid inside me with slow deliberation, an almost

painful tease of pleasure as he filled me. The stretch of him was so intoxicating, I could hardly bear it.

It had been a while for me. Long enough that the fit was tight. Remy's generous size didn't exactly help matters.

On the heels of a deep breath, he nudged forward slightly, and I cried out. Between the stretch of him and the pressure resting against my clit, I was already dancing along the edge of another release. All over again.

Chapter Seventeen

REMY

I felt as if I had tumbled into heaven. With Rachel's slick, tight heat surrounding me, clenching me, it was all I could do to maintain any control. Her skin was silky, and her curves soft and lush. Having all of her bare and warm underneath me was about as close to heaven as I could imagine. Not to be blasphemous, but it was the plain truth.

Her channel throbbed around me as her hips rocked restlessly into me. Her deep blue gaze was dark in the low lighting of her bedroom. I drew back slowly and sank inside again, a low groan escaping when she gasped, her body rippling under mine.

I meant to drag this out, to savor it. But I couldn't. It was too much, too good. I felt as if I was drugged with pleasure, with Rachel.

Her legs curled around my hips as she arched into me. Her nipples were taut and damp as they pressed into me, every point of contact searing my skin and spinning around my heart, cinching tighter and tighter.

"Fuck, Rachel, you feel so good," I murmured on the heels of another surge inside as her channel clenched my cock tightly, holding it exactly where it needed to be, buried deep inside of her.

She leaned up, her lips dusting hot kisses along my neck, every kiss sending jolts of lightning straight through me. Unable to hold back any longer, I rose up slightly and drew back. She took every inch as I buried myself inside her.

"Remy," she gasped.

She set the pace for us, restlessly shifting her hips until I was drumming into her. I could feel her quickening, her breath becoming ragged, her eyes dilated, and her pussy clamping down around my cock. Reaching between us, I pressed lightly on her clit and watched as she flew apart, gasping my name.

My own climax was already gathering inside, tightening at the base of my spine and then snapping through me like a bolt of lightning, the release so intense, I fell against her in the aftermath. Shifting my weight, I rolled us over until she was laying half on top of me while I was still buried inside of her.

She rested her head against my shoulder, her breath coming in soft gusts across my skin, the sensation tangling up inside of everything else coursing through me. My heartbeat slowed gradually as I held her fast against me. I didn't want to get up. *Ever.*

———

The following morning, I woke slightly disoriented. As the haze of sleep cleared, I reached reflexively for Rachel, instantly missing her presence when I realized she wasn't there. Rolling to my side, I saw the bathroom door was open and heard the sound of running water.

I knew exactly where I wanted to be. Kicking the covers off, I strode quickly into the bathroom. Rachel's form was blurry through the glass shower doors. My cock stirred at the thought of seeing her.

Opening the door, I stepped in to find bubbles rolling down over her curves and her skin flushed pink. Her sweet ass—and damn, she had a sweet ass—was the first place my eyes snagged.

"Mornin', sweetheart," I murmured as I slid my hands down over her wet curves.

Her answering squeak sent a surge of blood straight to my groin. I discovered last night that I fucking loved the sounds Rachel made. Rough cries, soft gasps, little whimpers, and bossy orders when she got impatient. That might've been my favorite part.

"Remy!" she exclaimed as she spun in my arms.

"Oh perfect." I immediately slid my palms up over the soft curve of her belly to cup her breasts. They were plump and heavy in my palms, her nipples immediately tightening when I brushed my thumbs across them, the soap making everything slippery and slick. "You sound surprised to see me," I added.

She drew back, her smile slightly bashful, paired with a naughty glint in her eye.

"A little," she admitted as her hand slid down and curled around my cock, which was standing at attention, more than thrilled to see her.

As soon as I heard the shower, I had it in my head I would be climbing in here and burying myself in her core. She took the reins right out of my hands. With a firm push of her palm against my chest, my back collided with the cool tile behind me as she shimmied down and promptly sucked my cock into her mouth.

"Fuck. Oh, Rachel." I groaned, one palm slapping against the tile as I threaded my other hand in her damp hair and hung on for dear life.

Her tongue slicked around the base of my cock as she drew up slowly, glancing through her wet eyelashes. She swirled her tongue around the tip, the sight alone almost making me come.

I tried to say something, but the only thing that came out was another rough groan. I have no idea how long she was sucking on my cock. All I knew was the feel of her, the warm suction of her mouth around me, her tongue driving me wild, and then my release pouring into her mouth. Drawing back, she licked her lips and grinned as she straightened. Meanwhile, I was barely managing to stand with the hot water pounding down over us. Thank fuck I had a wall behind me.

Somehow, I pulled it together and returned the favor. I was quite certain no man could resist Rachel's sweet pink pussy, or the sounds she made when I buried my fingers inside of her and teased her with my tongue. I would die a happy man if I died with those sounds ringing in my ears.

After we made practical use of the shower, Rachel made coffee and insisted on making me breakfast. I discovered last night she was an amazing cook, but I was fairly certain she made the best French toast I'd ever had in my life—light and fluffy with a dash of cinnamon, cardamom, and vanilla. Pairing that with rich dark coffee, and I was a contented man, all senses thoroughly sated.

The only problem? I actually had to leave. Rachel had to go to work, and I needed to get to the station. I wasn't due out for an overnight, but I did have a job, and unfortunately it didn't involve staying tangled up naked with Rachel for hours on end.

She chased me out of the kitchen, so I watched as she loaded the dishwasher, my heart thudding erratically in my chest. Looking for a way to collect myself, I glanced at the clock above the stove. Seven thirty a.m. I need to be at the station by eight. Slipping off the stool, I stood just as she closed the dishwasher and turned.

With her hair down, her skin flushed from our shower, and not a lick of makeup on, she was so damn sexy, she stole my breath.

"I gotta go," I said quietly.

She studied me for a few beats, and I wished I could see what the hell she was thinking. "I do too."

By some miracle, I managed not to tear her clothes off right then and there and take her in the kitchen. Between last night and this morning, I shouldn't have felt such fierce need. But I did, and there was no denying its force.

Chapter Eighteen
REMY

Later that afternoon at the station, I poured a fresh cup of coffee in the break room in the back, joining Jesse and Beck at one of the tables nearby. Like most stations, we had a fully outfitted kitchen, along with a combo rec room-living room that had two televisions. One was used for the guys who liked to play video games, and the other for watching shows. There was a large sectional couch and a number of reclining chairs. Beyond that area was a glass enclosed workout room. A hallway toward the back led to a couple of bedrooms, with another hallway leading toward the front offices.

We had several tables scattered in the kitchen area. I knew the rhythm of being a firefighter well. The main adjustment to being a hotshot firefighter was that most of our work ran from spring to autumn. We flew out wherever and whenever we were needed. In Alaska, Willow Brook Fire & Rescue served as a regional hub for three hotshot crews, all of which rotated, covering local duty for the town as well.

The station had one small local crew. The hotshot crews were twenty-five members apiece, so there was a large contingent here in town, although, only some crewmembers stayed here all year.

During the summer months, at any given point, two or three of the hotshot crews were called out to locations. We mostly served Alaska, yet we also flew anywhere we were needed, primarily in the western United States. Alaska was so large geographically, with such massive stretches of wilderness, there was plenty to do here in the summers. Alaska, like most of the West, had seen an uptick during fire season with hotter summers. The state also struggled with the aftermath of areas hit with spruce bark beetle, which had killed off large swathes of forest and created acres upon acres of fire fuel.

I took a sip of my coffee, glancing between Jesse and Beck. "So, what's our schedule for the rest of the week?"

Beck shrugged. "I was just arguing with Jesse over whether our crew would stay local for the rest of the week, or yours. We have a call out to do some more prep work outside Fairbanks in an area that got hit hard last year."

Normally, I would shrug and not care one iota. I loved my job and being out in the wilderness. But I was thinking tonight, I'd rather see Rachel again. I wasn't about to share that detail with these guys. Not now.

"When do we need to be out there?" I asked instead.

Jesse chuckled, rolling his eyes at Beck. "Not until next week. I call dibs staying next week. We've already traveled more this spring. In another month, it's going to be crazy busy."

Beck flashed a grin. "Fine, fine."

"Meet us at Wildlands tonight?" Beck asked as he stood from the table, draining the rest of his coffee.

"Oh yeah, I'll be there," Jesse replied. "Charlie already ordered me. I guess she'll be there with Rachel after they finish up at work, which means the rest of us better show up."

Beck chuckled as he strode over to the kitchen counter, putting his empty coffee cup in the dishwasher before heading to the hallway that led up front. "Exactly why I'll be there. I already have my marching orders from Maisie."

At the mere thought of seeing Rachel, anticipation shot through my body. "I'll be there," I replied, just as my phone vibrated in my pocket. Pulling it out, my sister's name flashed on the screen. "Catch y'all later, need to take this."

"Hey, Shay," I said as I stood from the table and brought the phone to my ear.

"Hey, hey, Remy," she replied, her tone cheery. "I was calling to see how your date went."

I'd completely forgotten I even told her I had a dinner date with Rachel. My mind flashed to the feel of Rachel clenching around me, the hazy look in her eyes with her skin pink and her lips puffy from our kisses.

I was close to my sister, but there was no way in hell I was going to share what came to mind with her. "Fine, Shay, it went fine," I replied with a little laugh. I walked toward the back area where it was quieter.

"Remy, you have to give me more than that," she protested.

What Shay wanted for me was to fall in love. With the way my heart sped at the thought of Rachel, for the first time in forever, I thought it might even be a remote possibility. But I wasn't ready to go there yet, not just now.

"Shay, you're my sister. You're only going to get so much," I said flatly.

Shay carried on. "Was it more than dinner?" she demanded next.

"Sweet Jesus, girl. Leave it alone. I'll be seeing her again. How about that?"

Shay's returning squeal had me pulling the phone away from my ear as I leaned against the wall toward the back. With the TV on and the other guys around the station largely occupied, no one was really paying attention to my conversation, but that didn't mean I didn't want a little privacy.

"That's enough," she said when she was done squealing.

"Maybe I should start asking you about your love life," I teased.

I meant for my comment to be light, just a joke, but I could feel Shay's pain radiating through the phone line.

"Hey, I didn't mean..." I began before she cut me off.

"I know you didn't mean anything, Remy. I should be able to handle teasing about my love life, or complete lack thereof. Plus, I'm on your case, so I guess I'm asking for it. On the subject of my love life, I was thinking of entering a convent."

"What?" I sputtered.

She burst out laughing. "Hey, I'm just being realistic. My dating prospects are abysmal. I swear like a sailor, I love to read romance, I've got gobs of baggage, and I'm pretty sure good sex is out of the question." Her last words contained bitterness.

For a moment, I didn't know what the hell to say to that, but I forged ahead anyway. "Hey, I support whatever you want to do. I don't want to hear about your sex life any more than you want to hear about mine. But if you want to be celibate and become a nun, I got your back. I just want you to feel okay and be okay."

My heart clanged inside. I felt generally helpless when it came to knowing how to navigate the tricky emotional terrain involving my sister and what her ex had done to her.

"I know you do, Remy," she said softly. "I'm okay. Dating really isn't on my radar right now, and I think that's definitely for the best. And if you want me to stop teasing you about dating, I will. It's just, you're one of the best guys I know, and I want you to find a girl who loves you."

"I know you do. I'll keep you posted. Good enough?"

"Absolutely. Love you, Remy. I gotta go."

"Love you, Shay."

Hanging up, I headed to the front of the station, wanting to ask Rex what else he could tell me about Bruce. If I had my way, somehow, he'd get chased out of town.

Chapter Nineteen

RACHEL

"Oh my God, I'm so tired," Charlie said, her hand resting on the slight curve of her belly as she sank into the chair beside my desk.

I hit save on the chart I was working on in our electronic record system and logged out. Spinning to face her, I smiled. "You look fucking gorgeous. You're one of those women who does pregnant really well. If I ever get pregnant, I'm pretty sure I'll hate you for looking this good."

Charlie sighed and gave me a smile in return. "You're just being nice. I'm not even that big yet, but it's the morning sickness that's making me miserable. It's not limited to morning for me." She sighed heavily.

I wasn't going to argue that point with her. I'd personally held her hair back when she had a rough bout of vomiting the other afternoon. But she *did* look absolutely gorgeous. Her skin was glowing, and she somehow managed to look great, even if she wasn't feeling too well at times. With her dark hair and gray eyes that somehow had a hint of violet in them, my best friend was gorgeous all on her own.

Her gaze sobered as she studied me. "I'm sorry I didn't know Bruce was out," she said softly.

We weren't the kind of friends to tiptoe around subjects. Thank God.

"Um, that's kind of a ridiculous thing to apologize for. It was just plain bad timing. The guy covering for Rex didn't know what happened. Between Rex being out of town and Maisie off, it was the perfect time for Bruce to show up in Willow Brook. No one was around who knew he beat the shit out of me," I said with a bitter laugh, tears hot behind my eyes.

"Hey," Charlie said softly. "Don't say it like that."

"Trying to pretend it wasn't as bad as it was doesn't help me. That's how I ended up backing into the whole mess with him anyway."

Charlie's mouth twisted to the side, and she leaned forward, catching my hand in hers and giving it a firm squeeze. "I'd hug you, but I don't feel like standing up."

I laughed. "I get it. We had a crazy busy day. You sure you want to go to Wildlands? You can't drink anyway."

Charlie shrugged. "I don't go for the drinks, but for my friends. Even though I'm tired, we need to go. Jesse is meeting us there, and you need to not be all up in your head."

After all was said and done, my friends pointed out they should've noticed I was making more and more excuses not to hang out with them. Part of that had been Bruce telling me who I could and couldn't see, but the other part had been me, as Charlie put it, all up in my head.

Conveniently, today Bruce happened to be far from my thoughts, for the most part. Instead, Remy had a starring role. After last night, I didn't know what the hell to think.

I didn't know what expression crossed my face, but Charlie narrowed her eyes and cocked her head to the side. "What's up?"

Instantly, my cheeks heated. "What do you mean?" I countered, attempting to gloss it over.

Charlie's eyes took on a gleam, and she arched a brow. "I don't know what I mean, but I know something's up. Spill it," she ordered.

You might think a pregnant woman who was graced with morning sickness and tired at the end of a busy day at work wouldn't come across as bossy. No such thing with Charlie. She commanded authority all on her own.

She was also a good friend, the best kind of friend. She knew when I needed to process things, and now was definitely one of those times. If I was going to tell anyone about Remy, I needed to tell Charlie. I took a deep breath and let it out with a slow sigh. My heartbeat sped up, even considering talking about Remy.

"All right, um, I spent the night with Remy," I blurted out. As soon as I said it, I realized that didn't even come close to capturing what had happened.

I startled Charlie so much she actually straightened in her chair, her eyes wide. "What? Did I miss a few steps along the way? Does spending the night mean sex?"

I bit my lip and laughed. "Yeah, I guess so. I haven't had a chance to say anything."

"Yes to spending the night means sex? Or yes to I missed a few steps?"

I sighed, feeling my cheeks heat. "Yes to both."

"Okay, I need details. *Now*."

"There's not a lot. I mean, he's totally hot, so there's always that."

Charlie nodded. "Yeah, Remy *is* hot. Don't think anybody's going to argue that point. More," she ordered, circling her hand in the air.

"Okay, so maybe two weeks ago, I ran into him when I was out for a run with Henry. I fell in the mud in front of him, so... Well, that was just a mess. Anyway, there was, I don't know, maybe a zing or something. Then, he asked me out to dinner, and I went. And then we made out. Then, he was gone and then he came back. He happened to be at the station yesterday after that thing with Bruce. I was all out of sorts and kind of emotional, and he came over and spent the night last night."

Through the jumbled mess of my explanation, when I said "then" a few too many times, Charlie's mouth slowly fell open, her eyes as wide as saucers by the time I was done. "You mean to tell me, you went on a date with Remy and didn't bother to tell me about it?"

"Yeah. I didn't see you for the last three days. Today's the first day," I said, scrunching my nose because I knew I could have called her.

Charlie drummed her fingertips on the armrest as she leaned back again. She pressed her other hand against her low back with a sigh.

"Can you take anything for that back pain?"

Charlie shook her head. "I'd rather not. It's not that bad. Jesse will rub my back later."

"Are you sure you shouldn't just go home instead of us going to Wildlands?"

"Hell yes, I'm sure. For starters, moving around a little bit actually helps. Plus, I'm texting Jesse in a sec and making sure that Remy will be there too. I need to see how he looks at you," she said as she fished her phone out of her pocket and started typing on the screen.

"You need to see how he looks at me?" I asked, genuinely curious as to what she meant.

"Yep, that's what I said. You're my best friend, and it's not cool if he just wants to fuck you."

"Hey, what if it's cool with me if he just wants to fuck me?"

The moment my question slipped out, my heart gave a funny little tumble in my chest. I couldn't forget how I felt last night. There was how crazy hot and delicious the sex was, but more than that, there was the intimacy that spun around us like gossamer silken threads.

Charlie was quiet for a moment. She took a deep breath and let it out slowly, her eyes narrowing. "Well, if you're okay with it, then obviously it's okay with me. Plus, you sure deserve good sex. Something tells me Remy can bring it."

I knew my cheeks were bright red all over again. "Definitely," I finally said, by some miracle keeping a perfectly straight face. I dissolved into laughter when she smiled slowly.

After a moment, her gaze sobered. "I don't know a lot about Remy."

Suddenly, emotion tightened in my throat and I wanted to cry. See, this was the thing that was so fucking awful. After being stupid enough to end up in a shitty relationship, I doubted my own judgment. Even worse, I knew my friends worried about me.

Catching Charlie's eyes, I shook my head. "You don't need to worry. I know Remy's not like that. I guess you might as well ask Jesse, though. I don't blame you for wondering about my judgment. Trust me, I do too."

"Sweetie, that's not what I meant," Charlie said.

When I shook my head, she sighed again. "Okay. I just worry. That's all. None of us realized Bruce was like that at first, so it wasn't just you. I just want you to be okay. Considering that you've been swearing off men for the rest of your life for the last year or so, I'm beyond thrilled to hear about Remy. Do I have your permission to be nosy and ask Jessie about Remy?" she asked softly.

"Of course you do. After what I went through with Bruce, I'm suspicious of any man. I don't know why I trust Remy, but I do."

"Honestly, my gut says he's a good guy. But I'm still going to be nosy. Is there anything else you didn't bother to tell me?"

I laughed, shaking my head. "No, I swear that's it."

"Okay, because I have to pee. Really bad."

"Oh God, you're not gonna piss your pants, are you?" I asked, leaping from my chair and rounding my desk.

Standing in front of her, I helped her up. Charlie shook her head once she was standing. "Not gonna ruin your chair. Even though what you were telling me was earth-shattering, I would've just made you come to the bathroom with me if I had to pee that bad. Be right back, and then we're going to Wildlands."

Chapter Twenty

RACHEL

I sat at a large round table in Wildlands, wondering if Remy would actually be here. Per a report from Charlie, who was sniffing out every detail she could learn about him from everyone already, Remy had told Jesse he would be here.

As if conjured by thought alone, he appeared from the back hallway. I happened to be seated in his line of sight, purely by chance. The moment I saw him, my pulse skittered and my belly flipped. From twenty feet away or thereabouts, his eyes snagged mine, and it felt as if a flame licked through the air across the room.

In a matter of seconds, he was pulling out the empty chair beside me. "Hey, sweetheart," he said, his slow drawl an aphrodisiac on its own.

"Hey." When his hand brushed my thigh as he pulled his chair in, I almost sighed aloud.

"Hey, man," Levi called from across the table.

"Hey there," Remy replied. A few more greetings were exchanged, and the waitress arrived. Remy ordered a beer and a burger with fries, looking over to my almost empty drink when the waitress asked if he needed anything else. "Need a refill, sweetheart? It's on me."

Tonight was half-price margarita night, and I usually only let myself have one drink. But Charlie had promised me a ride home, seeing as she couldn't drink. Conveniently, we lived quite close to each other, so she would also bring me to work tomorrow to fetch my car. With that in mind, I decided I didn't need to stick to my one-drink limit.

When I looked up at Remy, my heart stuttered and then lunged. Sweet hell. The man's eyes were just plain sex. His rich green gaze with heat flickering within had my belly somersaulting and my sex clenching.

"Sure, I'll take another margarita."

Given that we were staring at each other, it didn't even appear we'd involved the waitress in our conversation, but she chirped, "Got it. Anything else?"

Remy shook his head, never once looking away from me. "How was your day?" he asked when she moved on to check with someone else at the table.

"Busy. But I like busy, I don't like to be bored at work because then I just stare at the clock. Yours?"

"Same. I was hoping to run into you here."

"Oh?"

His lips kicked up at one corner, sending butterflies into a tizzy in my belly. "Yes. I was hoping to see you again tonight."

"Tonight?" I repeated, suddenly incapable of anything other than one-word responses.

"Yes, sweetheart. Tonight."

"Here?"

Even though Remy struck me slightly dumb, I also nudged at that sassy side of me, and this was fun.

"Yes, here. And preferably naked later," he said bluntly.

Heat flashed up my face, and I was relieved for the dim lighting in the bar. "Oh. Well then. I suppose that could be arranged."

"Excellent," he replied, just as his large palm curled over my thigh.

Damn. Remy had taught me one thing, quite thoroughly. I loved a man with big, strong hands. I regretted the fact we were anywhere public because I could think of all kinds of things I wanted him to do with his oh-so-talented hands.

My attention was drawn away when Maisie said my name. Glancing over, I asked, "Yeah?"

"I asked if you were going to get a dipnetting license this summer."

"Of course. I wouldn't miss it. I just have to decide where. The Kenai, the Kasilof, or China Poot," I replied, referencing two rivers and a small bay.

Dipnetting for salmon was a beloved activity for local Alaskans. It was as simple as it sounded—dropping a net in the water to catch the fish as they swam by. While Alaskan salmon of all varieties fetched a pretty penny at retail, residents could pay the fee for the dipnetting license and catch plenty of salmon. Fresh wild salmon straight out of Alaskan waters was a privilege few people got to experience. Being born and raised in Alaska, I knew I was spoiled rotten.

"Dipnetting?" Remy chimed in.

"Oh my God, you haven't been yet!" Maisie exclaimed. "Remy, you have to go. It's totally the best. I thought it was crazy when I moved here, and now I'd probably die without it."

Beck looped his arm over Maisie's shoulder, leaning over to press a kiss to her cheek. "My girl is hardcore. Another bonus to kids is we get extra fish for every kid."

"Oh, now that's a reason for more kids," Levi offered with a laugh.

Beck, proud father that he was, simply shrugged. "I think we're tapped out with two. But it is nice. That's fifty-five salmon. Last year, from the Kenai, we had over one hundred pounds. We still have a little bit leftover, although I bet we'll be out in another week or two."

Remy glanced to me, his eyes still puzzled.

"Okay, dipnetting is a type of fishing. But it doesn't involve a fishing rod, just a net. Now that you're a resident, you can get a license. You'll have to decide where because you can only get a license for one location. Everybody has an opinion on that, but they're all good, if you ask me. It's totally a blast, and you have to go. We usually plan a trip down together because parking is a nightmare."

Beck glanced to Remy. "Dude, it's combat parking."

"Well, I love salmon, so I guess sign me up. Where do I get my license?"

Conversation carried on as various opinions were bandied about for the best option for Remy's first year of dipnetting. None of us stayed late that night, not with Charlie looking as tired as she did. She gave me a few meaningful glances as the evening progressed, and I studiously ignored her.

With Remy's hand warm on my thigh and his fingers occasionally brushing along that crease near the apex of my thighs, I was in a bit of a state by the time dinner ended.

As the group gradually started to break apart and we were standing by the table, Charlie glanced my way. "You still need a ride?"

Remy's hand slid down my back as he answered for me. "I can take her home."

Before I even had a chance to reply, Charlie chirped, "Great. I'll see you tomorrow. I'll pick you up in the morning, okay?"

"You sure you don't mind giving me a ride?" I asked, glancing up to Remy. The heat banked in his gaze almost took my breath away.

"Absolutely not."

Dear God, the man could talk about the weather and turn me on. It was just a ride home, but he had me beyond hot and bothered.

With his hand warm on my back and his fingers brushing

over the curve of my bottom, we walked out together. My heartbeat was thudding so hard I could hardly hear over the sound of it.

When we stepped into the parking lot, the quiet enveloped us as the door closed. I gulped in a breath of the cool spring air, willing my body to calm down.

My body didn't listen. It appeared entirely uninterested in anything other than Remy and wondering how fast I could get him inside of me.

The tail lights of Charlie's car glittered through the almost darkness as she pulled out of the parking lot. A couple walked past us into Wildlands, the sound of the door shutting behind them loud in the quiet. Remy glanced down, reaching for my hand. His grip was warm and strong around mine as we walked toward his truck.

The lights from the lodge glimmered over the waters of Swan Lake behind the parking lot. A raven's call in the darkness was sharp, the sound of its wings beating through the air audible as it flew above us.

All the while, my pulse pounded madly and my breath was shallow.

As usual, Remy was quite the gentleman. He held the door of his truck open for me, making sure I was settled before closing it behind me. It was just all part and parcel of how he was. After Bruce had made a show of doing things like that when I first met him, I assumed I would be turned off by any man who did anything similar.

Not with Remy, not at all. With him, the sense of strength and protectiveness was so encompassing, I wanted to wrap myself in him. Nothing about him was for show. And yet, he was the most purely raw masculine man I'd ever known.

By the time Remy pulled up in front of my house, I was practically vibrating in the passenger seat. Desire was humming through my veins. He'd driven home with one hand on the steering wheel and the other resting on my thigh. Whether he meant to drive me crazy with lust, or not, I didn't know.

His touch was like a hot brand on me. The occasional, seemingly absentminded brush of his thumb across my thigh, right at the juncture of my hip, had turned me into a ball of need. My panties were soaked and my heartbeat fluttered. All the while, butterflies spun in my belly and my entire body tingled with fierce longing.

Chapter Twenty-One

REMY

Somehow, I managed to behave rationally. Which was saying something, considering I contemplated whether or not to just fuck Rachel in my truck when we stopped in front of her house. I'd been on fire since I first laid eyes on her tonight.

The only thing that stopped me was the sound of Henry's bark from the door. I knew he probably needed a bathroom break. Hence, why I opted against pulling Rachel into my lap and burying myself inside of her right this instant. With his second bark, she looked ahead toward her house, snapping her gaze from mine. We were simply staring at each other in the small cab of my truck.

The air was electric, the way it felt just before a storm hit. Heavy and laden with what was about to come. In this case, the lightning and the thunder were solely between us. We created our own damn weather system.

With lust beating like a drum through my body, I went through the motions, letting her out of my truck, walking up to the door, and even offering to take Henry out. I deserved a fucking medal for my restraint, or so I thought. Rachel stood beside me in the falling darkness. With the days getting longer and longer, I was discovering dusk lasted for hours here in Alaska.

"I came home at lunch and walked him today. I do that almost every day. When it's not too busy at the office, sometimes I bring him with me," she explained as she tossed the ball for him. Henry dashed down the small slope behind her house.

Glancing to her, I grinned. "Fetch is an easy way to make him tired."

As if to answer me himself, Henry raced back to us, promptly dropping the ball at my feet. Lifting the tennis ball, I threw it far, watching as his tail wagged with every step as he dashed into the trees.

"Exactly," Rachel replied. "A few more throws and we can bring him in, and he'll collapse. I like to run with him in the morning. That gets him tired enough that I assume he mostly sleeps when I'm not home." Henry returned with the ball, and I threw it again.

As we turned to walk back in a few minutes later, I reached down to adjust the front of my jeans. My cock had been hard for what felt like hours at this point. Rachel was solely responsible for my state. I wondered if she had any clue just how badly I wanted her.

After we returned inside and Henry gulped down some water, he selected his preferred chair in the corner and went to sleep. We happened to be standing by the kitchen counter. Reaching out, I caught Rachel's hand in mine and reeled her to me, letting out a groan when her soft body came against mine.

I was beyond finesse and didn't care to wait. "I need you," I murmured, right before bringing my lips to hers. They were soft, her mouth warm and sweet when I swept my tongue inside.

She sighed into my mouth, arching up to me, one hand sliding up over my chest and the other to cup my nape, her fingers teasing in my hair. Our kiss didn't start slow. It was like diving into fire—tongues tangling, gasps, and groans.

I needed to taste her, everything all at once. With a muttered curse, I broke free, gulping in air. Henry whimpered in his sleep, the sound of his tail wagging against the chair puncturing the haze of need in my mind.

"Bedroom. Now."

"Yes, please," she said with a little giggle as she nipped at my neck. The graze of her teeth sent a bolt of heat through my body.

Lifting her against me, I growled when she curled her legs around my waist, rocking her hips into my arousal.

"Damn, sweetheart, you're killing me."

I could feel the sweet heat of her through the denim of my jeans and her cotton pants. Tonight, she was wearing whatever she'd worn to work. It was completely practical, and on the surface, there was nothing sexy about it. Yet, on her, simple cotton scrubs were sexy as hell to me.

Shouldering through her bedroom door, I kicked it shut behind me before easing her down. Our clothes came off in a messy tangle. I wasn't thinking. At all. The single thought that repeated on a loop was *more, more, more*.

Everything was a blur, all sensation. Somehow, I found myself flat on my back on Rachel's bed, with her sitting astride me. Her slick pussy slid across my aching cock as she rocked her hips back and forth. Her blue eyes were bright in the dim light, and her nipples pink and damp from when I sucked on them moments ago.

My fingers dug into the generous curve of her hips. She slid back and forth again, shimmying back to lean forward and drag her tongue from the base of my cock to the tip, swiping up the drop of pre-cum rolling out.

"Sweetheart, I need to be in that sweet pussy of yours. Now," I ordered.

Rachel rose, a slow grin curling her lips as she looked down at me. "Wow, you're bossy tonight," she teased.

I wasn't even thinking. I had my cock in my fist and was lifting her up before I realized I didn't even have a condom on.

"Fuck," I muttered as I rolled to the side, wondering where the hell my jeans had fallen on the floor.

Her knees tightened on my hips. She was strong, just strong enough to stop my momentum. "Where the hell are you going?" Her eyes flashed as she looked down at me.

"Condom," I bit out.

Clearly, she had forgotten as well, her eyes widening. She held still for a moment, simply staring at me. "I'm on the pill. I don't know..." Her words trailed off when my breath hissed through my teeth.

She started to shift back, but I grabbed her tight again. "Are you sure?" I asked.

"Am I sure I'm on the pill?" she countered with a disbelieving laugh. "Of course I'm sure. I'm also clean. I'm a medical assistant, so I'm kind of on top of these things. I also haven't had sex for over a year. Well, not counting you."

I'd never had sex without a condom. But I trusted Rachel implicitly.

"I wasn't doubting you," I said, reaching up and brushing the messy tangle of her hair off her cheek. "I've never had sex without a condom, so it's a sure thing that I'm clean. But it's your call, not mine. That's why I was asking if you were sure."

We stared at each other for a long moment, and my heart squeezed in my chest. I didn't know what the hell *this* was with Rachel. Oh sure, the raw lust I felt for her transcended anything I had ever experienced by a long shot. But it was more than that, much, much more.

Something flickered in the depths of her eyes and then she settled her hips down again, sliding over my achingly hard arousal before rising slightly. Much as I wanted to take control, it was fucking hot as hell to let her take the reins.

Reaching between us, she held the head of my cock at

her entrance, almost sending me over the edge instantly. I could feel the sweet, wet heat of her kissing my cock. But I wanted more, and that alone helped me hang on.

She took me into her core slowly—inch by slick inch—until I was buried fully inside of her. I watched her through heavy eyes. She held still, and her gaze snagged with mine.

I couldn't help myself. I needed to taste her again. Leaning up, I caught her nipple in my mouth, giving it a hard suck and swirling my tongue around it before nipping lightly as I drew away.

Her sharp cry galvanized me. I gripped her hips, following her lead as she rose up and sank down. She took me inside of her slick, tight heat again and again and again. Her fingernails dug into my chest where her hand was resting. When she reached between her thighs and teased her fingers over her glistening wet clit while I drove inside of her, I lost it.

"So fucking hot," I groaned as my fingers dug into the soft give of her skin.

Her pussy throbbed and then clamped down around my cock as she flew apart, her head arching back with a rough shout of my name.

My own release followed immediately on the heels of hers. Pressure tightened in my balls and at the base of my spine. With an electric pulse, it let loose in a thundering wave through my body. She was so fucking tight, hot, and wet, clenching around me as my release poured into her.

She fell against me with a soft gasp, instantly tucking her head into the crook of my neck. My arms came around her, and I held on tight. My cock twitched with every shuddering clench of her pussy around me.

Closing my eyes, I breathed in the scent and feel of her surrounding me. After a few minutes, she dusted soft kisses on the side of my neck and rose up on an elbow, resting her chin on her hand on my chest.

It was an effort to open my eyes, if only because I was so

wiped out from that release. I didn't know how to read what
I saw her eyes, but my heart squeezed like a fist in reply.
Lifting a hand, I brushed a few damp locks of hair off her
forehead. We were both winded. Hell, I felt as if I'd run a
damn marathon.

She smiled softly and asked, "Are you staying?"

Chapter Twenty-Two

RACHEL

If you'll have me.

Remy's words echoed in my mind a few days later. As if I would ever have told him no. Sleeping with Remy was heaven. He was strong and warm and held me close all night. I knew this because he'd been there every night since then, and I was busy wondering if I was crazy.

People tell you things about how you'll know love when you feel it. You read about fairytales and think it'll never happen for you. You know, those silly stories about how you'll know right away when someone is *THE ONE*. All caps because, well, just because.

When I met Remy when he first moved to Willow Brook, I hadn't thought he was *the one*. But then, the first time I met him was only months after everything blew up with Bruce. My bruises had faded on the outside, but not on the inside. Those had been deep, so deep I still ached a little bit when I thought about it now, more than a year later.

I hadn't thought any man could be the one for me. I was quite certain no woman could be blind to Remy's charms.

The force of his presence was so potent and so powerful, I imagined a person could just feel it.

Now though... now, I knew what it felt like to be with him. I knew that feeling about thinking someone could be the elusive *One*. Whatever happened with Remy and me, I doubted I would ever feel this again. It was too rare, too special.

After what I'd been through before, I imagined actually trusting a man on that bone-deep level would've been largely impossible. Yet, that was how deeply I trusted Remy. It didn't make a lick of sense, because we hadn't known each other that long, not intimately.

I felt utterly and completely safe with him. So safe that when he was rather commanding when we were intimate, I loved it. Just thinking about it made my cheeks warm. Last night, when he slapped me on the ass and told me he wanted me bent over by the kitchen counter so he could make that fantasy come true, I hadn't even hesitated. I flung my T-shirt off, shimmied out of my jeans, and bent over.

The silk of my panties had been drenched, and he hadn't wasted much time getting rid of them before burying his cock deeply inside of me and leaving me boneless by the time it was over. So sated and weak, he had to carry me to bed.

Tomorrow was Friday, and I was thinking I wanted Remy to myself all weekend. To make matters worse, or better, depending on how you looked at it, it wasn't just the sex. The sex was incredible, beyond incredible. But it was more than that.

It was the fact that Henry adored him, and that Remy never made assumptions about me, or about what I wanted. It was the fact that while he could be so commanding, and frankly alpha, when we were intimate, his presence was like velvet steel. I knew he'd never hurt me. I knew he completely respected me.

Before Bruce, I hadn't encountered any man who sort of

swept me off my feet. In hindsight, what happened with Bruce wasn't that he swept me off my feet. Rather, he charmed me at first. Then, over the course of that first month with him, he discombobulated me and threw me off balance emotionally.

I confused that—that intensity, that sense of being overwhelmed—with the concept of falling for someone. Because I was terrified, and I hadn't known how to recognize it. I'd slow walked right into a disastrous, distractive relationship.

With Remy, I was also terrified, but for entirely different reasons. The only worry was that he might break my heart. This headlong rush into such emotional and sexual intensity left me feeling raw and vulnerable. The moorings inside keeping me emotionally safe had torn loose unexpectedly.

I had no idea how Remy felt about me. I knew he shared the same intense desire, and I sensed the intimacy between us. But I didn't know what it meant for him.

There was a sharp knock at my door and then it swung open. Glancing up, I found Charlie walking into my office. She slipped into the chair across from my desk and cast a teasing smile at me.

"So, who's Gavin Remy?" she asked.

"Huh?"

"Yeah, that last kid I saw. You know, the cute one with the missing front tooth? He broke his toe on the stairs?"

"Yeah, that was Gavin Stanton," I said slowly, quickly spinning in my chair and tapping the button to pull up my computer screen again. "I just entered his stuff in..." My words petered out when I realized I had actually entered his name as Gavin Remy.

I didn't even fight my blush when I looked back at Charlie. "Fine, so I may have gotten his name wrong. Fixing it right now," I said as I quickly corrected the last name and saved it.

Charlie's return grin was sly and knowing. "So, how are things with Remy?"

I smiled because I didn't really feel like hiding it. "They're great. I don't know what the hell it means, but I'm trying to do what you said," I explained, referencing a conversation we had the other day, "and just live in the moment."

"I gather 'the moment,'" she said, adding air quotes to the last two words, "involves Remy staying at your house every night now. Now, don't accuse me of going out of my way to be nosy. You know I have to drive by your house to get to work, so I've seen his truck there the last three days straight. You might want to know that I did my reconnaissance and apparently, Remy is a great guy all around on all reports. His parents died, which is really sad, and he's close with his sister. According to Jesse, he talks to his sister on the phone almost every other day. The guys all think he's awesome and he's lined up to take a foreman position soon, if he stays around. I even asked Rex to do a background check. Rex got a little pissy with me and told me I was being nosy. He pointed out that to get the job, Remy had to pass a background check, and he did. Jesse says Remy hasn't dated anyone since he moved to Willow Brook. So, as far as I'm concerned, you should fall in love and get married. You two would make beautiful babies."

I almost spit out the sip of coffee I had just taken. Charlie laughed and shrugged. "Sorry, maybe I'm getting ahead of myself, but you can't blame me. I have babies on the mind because mine is kicking a lot."

Snagging a few napkins out of my desk drawer, I wiped up the coffee splattered across my desk and shook my head. "I'll give you a pass, but yeah, you're getting ahead of yourself."

"Well, I want you to have someone. And Remy looks at you like he's going to eat you up, and it's totally hot."

Our conversation was interrupted with a quick knock and my door flinging open. Emily stood there.

"Hey!" Em announced as she strolled into my office.

Charlie turned to look at her with a wide smile. "Hey. Is it my imagination, or are you early?"

Em slipped into the chair beside Charlie, curling her knees up and resting her chin atop them. "Not your imagination. I finished my testing early and passed everything," she replied. Her following smile was shy.

I leapt up from my chair and raced around the desk to tug her up into a quick hug. "Yay! That's from me, and Charlie too. Because she's tired and we don't want to make her stand up," I said, as I squeezed Emily tight.

Em had a few rough years between her mom dying, her dad never being around, and moving to Alaska after her grandfather also died. To say the least, she'd been through some transition. She'd been really worried about her school exams and had confided in both Charlie and me about it. She was smart as a whip, and we knew she was going to do fine, if only her anxiety didn't get in her way.

When I drew back, Em's eyes were bright with tears. I bit back the urge to be sarcastic. With a friend, I might, but the fact that Em was even letting herself feel any emotion was too damn important for me to comment on it.

Charlie was standing and hugged her with a laugh. "I don't care what you think, but you're getting a hug."

Once the three of us were seated again, Em glanced between us. "Okay, your turn," she said, looking at me, her gray eyes so like Charlie's.

"My turn?" I countered.

"Uh-huh. Charlie hasn't mentioned it, but I'm not blind. I know Remy's been staying with you. Because I know what truck he drives and I've seen it there," she said with a sly grin.

Charlie burst out laughing. "Trust me, you can't keep secrets from teenagers."

My cheeks were flaming red. Dear God. It had never crossed my mind to think about the fact that Em's job at

Willow Brook Fire & Rescue meant she likely knew what every guy who worked there drove.

With a sigh, I shook my head. "No secrets from you, I guess. Well, we might be seeing each other," I finally said, uncertain how else to explain to a sixteen-year-old that I'd been having crazy, hot sex for the last three nights.

Em knew a bit about my history with Bruce. Not because I had chosen to tell her, but because Charlie had suggested we say something. With them living right down the road from me and passing my house daily, they'd been keeping an eye out if his truck showed up. The other issue was Charlie had come to see me in the hospital. It wasn't that I wanted to lie and cover anything up, but I'd been embarrassed as hell.

Plus, Bruce's arrest had been in our town's local paper. It wasn't as if she hadn't found anything out on her own. With my resigned agreement, Charlie had brought Em to see me in the hospital. She'd been a sweetheart and worried about me a lot. I didn't like to know she worried, but there wasn't much I could do to stop it.

Since then, she never asked me about guys. I knew she wondered, though, because she was a typical nosy teenager who had questions about everything.

Uncurling her knees, she tapped the toes of her boots against the back of my desk and cocked her head to the side. "I like Remy," she announced firmly.

"You do?" I asked, unable to keep from smiling.

Charlie nodded vigorously. "So she told me last night. In fact, Em thinks he's perfect for you."

Em giggled. "He is. He's totally a nice guy. He showed me how to do stuff with wheel bearings just last week. He's really patient and he knows everything. He's not a creeper, not at all. And I don't think he's dated anyone since he moved here last year. If he has, he's seriously on the down low," she explained, her eyes widening.

Charlie burst out laughing, right along with me. When I

got it under control, I met Em's eyes. "Well, I'm glad you like him. I do too."

Her smile faded, and she chewed on the inside of her cheek as she glanced between us. "I hope you like him. Because if he's spending the night, I'm assuming you're having sex. Both of you have lectured me about sex. Only have sex with someone you like. Only have sex if you feel comfortable. Don't have sex if you feel pressured. No matter what, it has to be on your terms," Em said firmly.

Charlie's mouth fell open, and she turned to look at Em. "Wow, you really do listen sometimes."

Em nodded firmly. "Uh, huh. I don't always do everything you say, but don't worry, I'm still a virgin," she said with a giant sigh. At that, Charlie and I laughed again.

"Thank God," I offered.

Em rolled her eyes and shrugged. "Whatever. After the stuff you went through, I think you deserve a guy like Remy."

Charlie looked from Em to me and winked. "See, just what I said."

Chapter Twenty-Three

RACHEL

The following night, for the first time in four days, Remy wasn't here. I threw the ball for Henry who dashed off after it. I missed Remy.

You're being a little ridiculous. You and him are fresh, like really fresh, and you still have no idea if he feels anything even remotely like you do.

I shook my thoughts away. My mocking voice had quite a lot of practice in the aftermath of Bruce spinning through my life, leaving a trail of wreckage, crushed confidence, and shattered self-worth in his wake.

The only reason Remy wasn't here was because he was with his crew at a training up in Fairbanks. Apparently, they were going to work with a couple of the other hotshot crews up there, for training for some of the newer crewmembers in a few fire-prone areas in the wilderness.

It wasn't like he was blowing me off. In fact, he only left this morning after a knee-weakening kiss turned into a quickie on my kitchen counter.

Henry came dashing back, dropping the ball at my feet. After another throw, Henry let out a sharp bark, his fur

bristling as he came to a stop at my side. His attention was
focused toward the front of the house.

Instantly, the hair on the back of my neck rose and my
stomach tightened into a knot, a sense of nausea rising in my
throat. I knew without knowing that Bruce was here.

I slipped my phone out of my pocket. I didn't even want
to turn around, but I knew I had to. Henry stayed right
beside me. I wanted to cry because I felt like my dog was
braver than I was.

Turning, I noticed Bruce's truck right away. I hadn't
recognized it before because it wasn't the vehicle he had
before he went to jail. Back then, he had an old beater of a
truck. This SUV was black with tinted windows. I hated it.

I dialed nine-one-one, lifting the phone to my ear as I
remained where I was. I wasn't going to give Bruce the satisfaction of walking over there and asking him to leave. That's
how Bruce was. He got off on manipulating situations like
that. I imagined he would claim I hadn't even told him to
leave.

Swallowing through the tightness in my throat, I ignored
the fear beating like wings in my chest, hurting all the
bruised places in my heart that I kept hidden away.

Maisie's familiar voice answered. "Nine-one-one, what's
your emergency?"

I took a deep breath, trying to speak. Maisie continued
before I even managed to get through the gravel in my
throat. "Hey Rachel, don't get all paranoid. Your number just
showed in my locator. Is Bruce there?" she asked, her tone
calm and somehow soothing.

Staring at his SUV, I finally managed to speak. "Yeah,
he's sitting at the end of my driveway, blocking it."

"I'm assuming you're alone because Remy is out in Fairbanks with his crew, right?"

"Uh-huh. Guess I can't keep anything private, huh?" I
tried to laugh and make a joke of it, but all I wanted to do
was cry.

"Rex is already on his way, along with backup," Maisie replied calmly. For the moment, she ignored my failed attempt at humor. "You're staying on the line with me until he gets there, okay?"

"Don't worry, I won't hang up. I don't think Bruce plans to get out. He's playing one of his bullshit games where he wants me to come up and tell him to leave. Everything for him is a game," I said bitterly.

"Of course it is. But you're fine. Rex should be there in less than a minute. Where's Henry?"

I reached down to stroke my hand along his back. "He's right beside me. He's not happy. He's never even met Bruce, but somehow he knows he's not a good guy, even from a distance."

"Rex said to tell you he's not coming in with the sirens on. He doesn't want to give Bruce a chance to take off. This is a clear violation of the restraining order, so he'd like to observe Bruce right there."

"Good plan. How the hell do you know all that already?"

"We have a chat feature where I type in everything. He was over near your area when you called anyway."

"Oh, okay. So, how's your day going?" I asked, searching for something to say other than to stand here in silence and hold onto the phone, as if the phone itself was going to save me.

"It's okay. I'll be better when I know Rex is there."

"He's here," I said, the moment I saw the police cruiser appear on the road.

"Stay with me until Rex is out of his car, okay?" Maisie asked.

"You know, you're kind of bossy for a dispatcher," I teased. The relief at having Rex here and knowing I wasn't alone was so immense, I was torn between wanting to burst into tears, or laugh so hard that I lost my breath.

Rex lifted his hand in a wave as he pulled up behind Bruce and climbed out of his car. In a split-second, Bruce gunned it, gravel spitting from his tires. I was surprised Rex had actually gotten out of his car, but I shouldn't have been. In a matter of seconds, his backup went flying by on the road, hot on Bruce's heels.

I was surprised Bruce stayed in my driveway as long as he had, knowing he could see me on the phone. But then, Bruce was somehow both wily and stupid. When presented with an opportunity to attempt to establish dominance, he took it, to hell with the potential consequences.

I approached the front of the yard, meeting Rex halfway down my driveway. Henry circled him with soft yips and his tail waving like mad.

Rex stroked his hand over Henry's head in greeting. "I'm gonna take off after my guy. I got my other guy on the far end of your road, so Bruce isn't going anywhere. You okay?"

I nodded jerkily, trying to take a deep breath but not getting much air. "Nothing happened, except he parked at the end of my drive. I don't know what he's thinking. I thought he was with somebody else."

"He's still living with his new girlfriend," Rex said with a nod. "I'm keeping tabs on him. Guys like him, though, nothing gets to them more than a woman who actually leaves. I already called the D.A. She's filing charges for a violation of the restraining order. It's a no-brainer because I saw him here."

Rex was quiet for a moment, looking to the house to Henry and then to me. "If Remy was in town, I'd tell you to make sure he was around tonight. Even with charges, there's a damn good chance Bruce'll bail out tonight."

I nodded. "I'm supposed to have dinner with Charlie tonight, so I'll be down there."

Chapter Twenty-Four

REMY

The plane angled in the sky, and I looked out into the distance where Denali stood tall, a sentry in the landscape. The snow line was gradually inching higher on the mountain. It would hold snow on its peak all year long, while the snow on its flanks would rise slightly as it melted during the warmer weather.

I recalled the first time I'd flown out with the crew last autumn. The stunning Alaskan wilderness was mind-blowing —miles and miles and miles of raw beauty. Mountain peaks and ridges, lakes and rivers, swathes of forest, and, closer to the coast, glaciers sparkling ethereal blue. As the plane turned toward Willow Brook, Swan Lake became visible in the distance, glittering under the late afternoon sunshine.

I loved my job. I always had. When I did my firefighter training back in North Carolina, I thrived off the sense of urgency, the sense I was doing something that mattered. My father had been a volunteer firefighter while I was growing up. That was what had originally had me marching down to sign up for the volunteer training right after I turned eighteen. I stayed on as a volunteer through college in western

North Carolina. When all was said and done, my college degree wasn't worth much because I accepted a position immediately as a full-time firefighter.

I enjoyed that for a few years and then wanted to spread my wings into hotshot training. We didn't have as many wildfires in the East, if only because of the differences in terrain and natural risks. Everything I loved about being a firefighter, combined with my love of the wilderness, sated part of my soul.

For the last three days, our crew joined forces for combination training and working exercises in a few areas within short flight distances from Fairbanks. Wildfires were risky, particularly near the more settled areas. We did a controlled burn and worked on clearing sections to help with management during the summer.

Normally, I didn't miss anyone when I was away. The old pangs of grief from my parents' death were ever-present, and I always missed Shay. But these last three days, Rachel had sashayed through my thoughts whenever I had a minute to think. I fell asleep with her winding through my dreams and woke to her front and center first thing in the morning.

The sight of Denali let me know Willow Brook wasn't too far away. I hoped I could see Rachel tonight. Yet, things between us were new enough that I didn't know if that was a given. I hoped like hell it was.

Slipping my phone out of my pocket, I powered it up, wondering if we were close enough to civilization to get reception. A whopping single bar showed, but that was enough for a text.

Hey, I'm landing with the crew shortly. Hoping I can see you tonight. Missed you.

My thumbs hesitated over those last two words, but I typed them anyway. I might not have planned for Rachel to spin into my life, but it didn't change the fact I wasn't about to let her go without making sure she knew what she meant to me.

My heart tightened when the plane angled into a turn, and I could see the streets of Willow Brook taking shape ahead, a tiny map from the sky. Willow Brook was about an hour slightly west and north of Anchorage. With the ocean glimmering in the distance, Swan Lake centered smack in the middle of town, and the trees giving way to an opening in the foothills, a tension I hadn't noticed I was carrying eased slightly.

As our pilot, Fred, lowered the plane slowly with the runway of Willow Brook's small airport coming into view, I felt my phone buzz in my pocket.

Hey, of course I'm free tonight. Call me when you land.

That was just enough to set anticipation humming through my body. She didn't reply to my comment about missing her and then I saw the little bubbles appear on the screen.

Missed you too.

Emotion tightened in my chest. I hadn't realized I'd been waiting.

After a steaming hot shower in the locker room at the station, I changed into clean jeans and a navy blue T-shirt. I had already called Rachel, planning to head straight to her place after picking up a pizza. She told me she had a busy day at work and hadn't had time to get groceries to make anything for dinner.

There was something so damn mundane about it all, and I loved it. While waiting a few minutes for the pizza to be ready before I left to pick it up, I rested my elbow on the counter surrounding Maisie's desk. Levi was betting with Beck on who could get home sooner.

Rex came out of the hallway on the police side of our shared station. He glanced amongst us and smiled. Pausing beside me, he commented, "Good to have you back. Seeing Rachel tonight?"

"Yeah, not that it's any of your business," I replied.

Rex rolled his eyes. "Trust me, I don't give a damn about your love life. But Bruce showed up at her house the other night. We arrested him and charged him with violating the restraining order. He posted bail and got released the same night. Far as I know, he hasn't been back out there, but I'll be damn relieved if she's not at home alone. I know she's got her dog, but..." Rex's words trailed off, and he shook his head.

Levi and Beck had meandered out to the parking lot to look at Levi's new truck. Maisie glanced up, her eyes bouncing from me to Rex and back again. "Don't worry, we're all looking out for her," she said.

As the primary dispatcher here, Maisie was usually up to speed on any police contacts. Anger coursed through me. "What the fuck? How is it okay for him to pull that shit and stay around town? Plus, I thought he had a new girlfriend."

Rex shrugged, his mouth twisting. "No matter what people do, it doesn't mean they can't live somewhere. Trust me, I wish the asshole didn't live here, but he does. And yeah, he's got himself a new girl and charges related to her too. Just like I told Rachel, I'll tell you. Even with a new girl-friend, guys like him take it *real* personally when a woman actually ups and leaves like Rachel did. He's not the brightest bulb, but I think he gets that he isn't going to get Rachel back. That doesn't mean he doesn't wanna make her uncomfortable. He just wants to fuck with her. That's how I see it."

"Rachel's going to be fine," Maisie said firmly. "Don't get me wrong, I'm glad she's got you now, but she's one of the strongest women I know."

If she intended to say anything else, she was interrupted by the dispatch line. Spinning away, she took the call.

Glancing to Rex, I nodded. "Thanks for letting me

know." I didn't know what else to say. I wanted to hunt Bruce down and beat the hell out of him, but I certainly wasn't planning to share that with Rex.

Rex nodded slowly. "Don't do anything stupid, okay?"

"You mean, like kick her ex's fucking ass?"

"Exactly like that."

"I'm not stupid, but I can't make any promises. I'll leave it at this, though. It'll definitely be something he starts."

Chapter Twenty-Five

REMY

Rachel stood in front of me, her hair loose and cheeks flushed. I'd arrived at her house a while ago to find her playing fetch with Henry in the yard. I stayed outside with her, wanting to ask about Bruce, but unsure how she'd feel about that.

Between the lust that jolted me anytime I was near her and the intensity of my feelings for her, worrying about the bullshit Bruce was pulling had me tied up in knots.

We'd just come inside a few minutes prior. The sound of Henry lapping water from his bowl was in the background as I looked at her. "I heard about Bruce." My mouth got ahead of my brain. Fuck.

Rachel's eyes widened. She was silent long enough that I knew I shouldn't have said anything.

"What did you hear?" she asked softly.

"Rex mentioned Bruce was here. He told me he arrested and charged him, but that Bruce was already back out."

Emotions flashed across her face—frustration, sadness, regret, anger. Underneath it all, that sense of vulnerability flickered.

She caught the corner of her bottom lip, worrying it. She twirled a loose lock of hair around her finger and tapped her foot, her body practically vibrating from nervousness.

I wanted to pull her into my arms and hold her tight. Because of everything Shay had gone through and because I'd come to know Rachel, I guessed she felt ashamed, that maybe she thought she should've known better, or she assumed just about everyone judged her for ending up in that situation. Perhaps all of it tangled together.

When none of it was true. Much as I wanted to argue the point, I also knew from Shay that all I could do was show that wasn't the case through my actions.

The steely look in Rachel's eyes faded, and her breath came out in a soft puff as her shoulders slumped forward. She looked defeated, and I hated it. She took a step back from where we stood near the kitchen counter. Sliding her hips onto a stool, her mouth twisted to the side, bitterness flashing in her gaze.

"It sucks. It totally sucks. I mean, he's got a new girl-friend. Why keep bothering me?"

Staring at her, I spoke the plain truth, at least the truth as I knew it in my heart. "Because men like that are fucking assholes. It's not about logic, or what makes sense. It's about power and control. Look, I don't talk about it much because it's not my story to tell, but like I said, my sister went through something similar."

Rachel's eyes held mine, sadness flickering in the depths again. "Too many women went through something similar. It makes me sick. You said she's okay, right?"

My heart squeezed just thinking about what Shay went through. "Yeah, she's okay. She swears she's never going to date again now."

Rachel let out a bitter laugh. "I was saying the same thing. And then you came along."

Rachel, usually guarded, looked bashful and vulnerable

for just a flash, just enough to set my heart to thudding against my ribs.

"Are we dating then?" I asked softly.

The feeling in the air around us shifted rapidly. The space felt electric, like a live wire shimmering in the air, vibrating hot and steady.

Rachel's cheeks flushed pretty and pink, and her eyes darkened, answering the desire I knew was contained in mine.

"I don't know. But I swore off sex, and you made me break my promise really fast," she said with a husky laugh.

Stepping closer to her, between the cage of her knees, I lifted my hand, brushing a few tangled locks off her cheek and threading my hand into her hair. My thumb brushed along the side of her neck.

"I'm so fucking glad you broke that promise." I could feel her tight nipples against me, and lust lashed inside, the sting of it sharp. "I don't know what you're thinking, but this is more than sex to me."

Rachel was quiet. I could feel the rise and fall of her breath as her breasts pressed against me. Henry padded across the floor and leapt onto the chair in the corner, promptly sighing into sleep.

Rachel's tongue darted out, swiping across her bottom lip and sending a hot shot of blood straight to my groin. I didn't quite know how this feeling between us had built so rapidly, but I didn't doubt it.

It was everything, and I wanted to shout it to the world, or at least to her. Yet, I knew how skittish she was. I knew how much it took for her to let down her guard. So, I would wait until she let me know it was okay to be that direct. In words, that is.

In these moments, intimacy wound around us like gossamer ribbons.

"Me too," she finally said, her words so soft I almost missed them.

Then, she slid her hand around my hips, nudging me just a little bit closer. I closed the distance between our lips, catching hers in a hot, wild kiss. I was beginning to realize the moment I was close to Rachel like this, there was no such thing as control. At least, not how there usually was when it came to women and sex.

Her mouth was warm and mobile, her tongue tangling sensually with mine. The little soft gasps and whimpers from her throat drove me fucking wild. I groaned when I slid a hand over her belly, growling when I cupped her breast and teased a tight nipple with lazy strokes of my thumb. Time dissolved when I was with her, everything blurring.

She broke free from our kiss, her lips, teeth, and tongue blazing a fiery trail down the side of my neck as she tugged at my T-shirt. Lifting her head, she ordered, "Shirt off. I need to feel you."

"Sweetheart, I'll do whatever you say." Reaching behind my neck, I lifted my T-shirt up and over my head. As it drifted to the floor, she pulled her shirt up and got her hair tangled.

With her shirt halfway over her head, I had an absolutely delicious view of her breasts pressed together, her nipples taut through the navy blue silk of her bra. Leaning forward, I sucked a nipple into my mouth, straight through the silk.

She gasped and then muttered with a giggle, "A little help, please."

Reluctantly drawing back, I made quick work of her T-shirt. She flicked open the buttons of my jeans, eliciting a rough growl from my throat when she freed my cock from my briefs and curled her palm around it.

"Sweetheart, I..." My words were lost in a ragged cry as she dipped her head and swirled her tongue around the head of my cock, taking care of the pre-cum rolling out the tip.

"You were saying?" she teased.

At the sound of her husky voice, I looked down. Her hips were still resting on the stool, but she'd shimmied back a little and was leaning over. Her breasts were on glorious display for me. I had a perfect view of the valley between them and one of her nipples peeking over the silk.

Reaching forward, I took care of matters, flicking my thumb on the clasp between them. "Fucking perfect," I murmured as her breasts tumbled loose. Capturing one in my palm and rolling her nipple between my thumb and forefinger, I savored the hiss of her breath between her teeth.

Her eyes had that hazy look I loved. Rachel was a woman almost always in control, so it made it that much more meaningful when she teetered on the edge. I fucking loved the surge of power that roared through me realizing I could make her lose control. Even more though, I loved knowing she felt safe to let down her guard with me. It was a gift. One I would never take for granted.

"I bet your pussy is fucking wet as hell," I murmured.

She shifted her thighs, a sly gleam entering her eyes. "Maybe so, but you're gonna have to wait."

At that, she leaned forward and sucked me all the way to the back of her throat. My hand slapped on the counter as I groaned, tangling the other hand in her hair and hanging on.

She licked, she stroked, she sucked. Making me fucking crazy. Her mouth and tongue worked magic on my cock.

I meant to tell her I wanted to be inside of her. Thought fled, my climax weakening my knees and roaring through me. If I hadn't been holding onto the counter, I'd have fallen. Rachel took it all, every last drop of my release poured into her mouth.

She drew back slowly. At the sight of her, her lips puffy and damp from sucking me off, her eyes dark with passion, and her cheeks flushed, my cock stirred again instantly. As she rose up, I kissed her. Because I had to. I tasted the salty evidence of my release on her tongue, and I loved it.

Chapter Twenty-Six

RACHEL

Remy lifted me, and I curled my legs around his hips. There was something about a man with such easy strength. When Remy held me, I knew he'd never let go. He held me with his strong arms high against him, his body a haven and a bulwark against anything.

One of his big hands sifted through my tangled hair as he murmured against my temple, "I need to be inside you, sweetheart."

He carried me, striding quickly into my bedroom and kicking the door shut behind him. In a matter of seconds, he eased me down and nearly yanked my jeans off. They caught on one of my ankles, and I stumbled.

He steadied me at the hip, kicking his own jeans free. My mouth went dry. He was all man. Tall and fit, every inch of him put to good use. We'd been together enough now that I was familiar with the map of his body, and the few scars here and there—a jagged one cross the back of one of his upper arms, a long one across his back, which he told me happened when he was a little boy playing on a rope swing. The rope caught under his arm and whipped across his back.

I loved these details, each of them adding up to more of the man standing before me. Remy was one of the strongest men I'd ever known, and one of the gentlest.

In a flash, we were on the bed, a tangle of skin, and his hands were everywhere as he mapped my body. Teasing my nipples, grazing with his teeth, just enough of a bite that it blurred into pain, and I savored it. There was a rough edge to him. Or perhaps, there was a rough edge to *us*. The need was so great, it seemed nothing could slake it. It ebbed and flowed like the tide, flashing like storms in the sky.

I felt the scratch of his stubble on the inside of my thigh, one of his palms pushing my knees apart. His fingers dipped into the core of me. I was gripping his hair and crying out as he fucked me with his fingers and tongue, bringing me to a rough, noisy climax.

It was always like this with him. I never wanted it to end, and yet it crashed over me so fast because it was so intense. Not to mention, the man was a fucking god in bed.

As he started to rise up, I caught him with my knees, rolling us over so I sat astride. My juices were slick on his cock. I rocked my hips, loving that he was already hard again. I meant to tease him, but I teased myself, sweet pleasure radiating from my clit as his hardness slid over the swollen button.

I wasn't thinking. At all. Rising up, I started to reach between us because I needed him inside of me, needing him stretching me and filling me completely. Suddenly, he was gripping my hips tightly. "What?" I asked, looking down.

"Take it slow," he murmured.

It felt as if he looked straight into my heart. Emotion tightened in my chest, and I felt restless, almost fearful of the depths he understood so effortlessly.

Just now, so alive with sensation, tingling from head to toe with my body practically beating out Remy's name with every fiber, all I wanted was him.

"Okay," I whispered, swallowing through the thickness in my throat.

With his hands gripping my hips, I eased down over him slowly, moaning at the delicious stretch of him filling me. He was thick and hard and filled me completely.

"Rachel."

My name was a gruff sound in the room, sending a prickle of awareness chasing over my skin. Opening my eyes, I looked down at him, his green gaze dark and intent. There was a slight sheen of sweat on his skin, just as there was on mine. The feel of his calloused palms against my skin was something I had come to savor. He shifted his hands, sliding them onto my thighs where the skin was so sensitive.

"I just want to see you," he murmured, answering my unspoken question.

I rose slightly, loving how his hips arched up to meet mine. With him propped on the pillows, I angled forward, pressing my lips to his. I couldn't look away. We rocked into each other, a slow, sensual dance that unraveled me inside—physically and emotionally. My release was crashing over me, and I was crying out, his name a broken shout. He went taut under me, and I felt the lustrous heat of his release filling me.

His palm slid up my back, pulling me to his chest where I collapsed against him. We stayed like that, and I simply floated in a haze. I was warm in his arms and never wanted to move.

Eventually, I heard a rustling at the door. "Henry," Remy murmured into my hair.

"He probably needs his after-dinner bathroom break," I said with a little laugh, pushing up slightly.

"I'll take care of it. If that's okay with you," he said, arching a brow in question.

"Of course."

We untangled ourselves, and I enjoyed the sight of

Remy's ass as he stood to tug on his jeans, not even bothering with a shirt, even though it was decidedly chilly out.

I fell asleep later with Remy curled warm around me, and
Henry at the foot of the bed. I'd never felt so safe in my life.

And that terrified me.

Chapter Twenty-Seven

RACHEL

I came awake slowly, burrowed against Remy's warm, strong body. Even in sleep, he exuded strength. Lifting my head, I glanced down to see Henry sacked out at the foot of the bed, tucked into a little spot in the crook of Remy's bent knee. A smile curled my lips.

Remy was still sound asleep, his chest rising and falling slowly, and I took a moment to simply look at him. His dark blond hair was mussed from sleep. He had an arm holding me close, and a hand resting on his chest. His thick lashes curled against his cheeks. Even in sleep, he was too damn handsome. I trailed my fingertips lightly over the sculpted line of his cheekbone and down along his jawline, the stubble prickling against my fingers.

His face was all clean, strong lines with those full, sensuous lips. I couldn't resist and let my hand trail down along his collarbone, nudging the sheet down carefully. My breath quickened and my pulse kicked up a notch. His chest was a work of art, nothing but hard, muscled planes.

I felt his gaze on me as his breathing shifted. Whipping

my eyes up to him, heat flooded my cheeks when his mouth curled in a slow, sleepy grin.

"Mornin', sweetheart," he drawled. "Enjoying the view?"

I shrugged, striving for nonchalance. "Maybe," I teased, letting my palm slide across his chest.

He reached over, casually cupping my breast and teasing his thumb across my nipple, which immediately puckered tight. I was suddenly hot all over, but then, Remy made me hot all over *all* the time.

He leaned up, dusting kisses along the side of my neck, each point of contact sending a sweet *zing* of electricity through me.

"Henry's here," I gasped when he nipped the side of my neck and shivers chased across my skin.

Remy's low chuckle sent my belly into a spinning flip. He rose up on an elbow, the sheet sliding down to his waist and giving me an excellent view of his cut abs. I couldn't resist dragging my hand down, and his gaze slid to mine. "Watch it. You're the one who pointed out we had an audience."

I giggled. Henry, roused from his dog sleep, lifted his head and gave it a little shake, his ears flopping wildly. Otherwise, he didn't move, looking back and forth between Remy and me.

My eyes flicked down to see Remy's arousal tenting the sheets. My mouth watered and my hands itched to reach down and touch him. I knew just how he would feel—warm and hard, the skin velvety soft.

But I couldn't, not with Henry staring at us expectantly.

"Shower," Remy said firmly.

Kicking the sheets off, he rose from the bed, entirely unselfconscious and glorious in his nudity. As I shifted to roll over and follow him, I became acutely aware of the slick heat between my thighs.

I'd never been one to think quickies were worth it. But then, I'd never been with a man like Remy. In a matter of seconds, Remy was sliding into me from behind. I slapped my palms against the shower wall and thanked God Remy had a firm grip on me. Without him, I was certain I'd have melted to the floor. He sent me flying with the heat of his release filling me.

It was so raw, so elemental, I was left reeling afterwards. He kissed me with the water pouring over us.

A short while later, as I started scrounging something up for breakfast, he took Henry out for his morning walk and fetch. My heart kept pounding, while anxiety spun through me. Because, you see, I loved this. Every single minute of it.

I could handle the good sex with Remy. He was all kinds of sexy. Yet, I was unprepared for the way his strength would call to me, and the way his gentleness tempered that very strength.

We had coffee and I made scrambled eggs with bacon for breakfast. We left my house together, with Remy following behind me into Willow Brook until he turned off at the station, and I kept going to my office.

I was falling in love, and I was crazy to let it happen.

Chapter Twenty-Eight

REMY

I took a sip of the coffee in the kitchen at the station and grimaced. Glancing to Levi, I said, "Damn, man, this stuff's got to be hours old. You coulda warned me."

Levi chuckled. "I guess I'm more desperate than you. I didn't sleep a fucking wink last night. Well, that's not true. Maybe I cleared a full hour in fifteen-minute increments," he replied with another healthy gulp of what I knew to be shitty coffee.

"Glory keeping you up?" I asked as I poured out what little was left of the coffee, rinsing the pot, and starting a fresh pot. Levi and Lucy had a little baby girl only months ago.

Levi nodded, taking another gulp of his coffee. "Yeah, and Lucy's got a cold. Not that she slept much more than me because she's miserable with coughing, but yeah, I'm fucking tired. Too tired to make a fresh pot of coffee, so thanks for that. How are things with you?"

"Well, I slept last night, so I'm a step ahead of you." I turned and rested my hips against the counter running along the wall while we waited for the coffee to brew.

Levi cracked a weary smile in return as I considered that I slept like a damn baby last night. Rachel was responsible for that. I'd come to appreciate sleep. It had been fleeting at times over the past few years. Grief did funny things. Stealing sleep was yet another box I could check of the things I lost when grief crashed over my life in waves.

But I found sleep easily with Rachel warm beside me and a sense of pure contentment spinning through me. Once I'd woken, I buried myself in her sweet heat all over again.

Yet, I'd seen the anxiety flickering in her eyes this morning and knew I needed to take this at her speed, much as I wanted to rush it. I figured something out, damn quick, when it came to Rachel. She was the one and only woman for me.

Years back, when I was nothing but a horny teenager, my dad told me I would know when I met the right woman, and I would be willing to fight for her. I knew my parents had a good thing. Until I met Rachel, I hadn't quite understood what he meant. She was *it*. She was *everything*. She was also feisty and scarred underneath it all.

So, I'd bide my time, even though it would be the hardest damn thing I'd ever done.

Levi cut into my thoughts. "I know you just made the coffee, but mind if I have the first cup? Before the pot's full?"

When I looked into his bleary eyes, I took pity on him. "Of course not."

He flashed me a smile. Turning, he slipped the coffee pot out and filled his mug quickly before returning it. He took a slow swallow, letting out a grateful sigh. "Pretty sure you make the best coffee out of everybody here."

"Hell yeah, he does," Harlow May replied as she strode by from the back of the station.

Harlow was one of two female firefighters at the station. She and Susannah were close. Like every single female firefighter I had ever worked with, they both more than held their own and probably had more nerve than all the men combined.

But then, my dad had always told me women were stronger than men, so it only made sense.

"Oh, you think?" I countered, catching Harlow's eye.

She grinned. "I think so. My coffee's adequate, but it's nothing amazing. The rest of the guys are chumps when it comes to coffee. Well, except for maybe Levi." Harlow kept on walking with a wave.

I idly watched her walk down the hall, her dark hair pulled up in a ponytail, and her hips swinging with her steps. I considered I should think she was beautiful, and I did, but from a purely objective perspective. Yet, I felt nothing, not even the slightest interest.

Whatever I was about to think in that moment was drowned out with a call over the intercom. "Police need backup..."

Levi started to push off the counter, and I shook my head. "I got it, I'll grab Beck and we'll go."

Whenever we were handling local duty for minor calls, whoever was available at that moment took care of it, depending on how many were needed. Within minutes, Beck and I were headed out to what had originally been a domestic disturbance call. After the police arrived, a man yanked out the propane line, creating a risk of fire.

Beck glanced over from where he was driving the truck, his eyes narrowing. "You know where we're going, right?"

"I know the address, if that's what you mean."

"It's Rachel's ex. This is where he lives with his girlfriend."

"You're fucking kidding me."

"Nope. Maisie just mentioned it to me on our way out. You cool?"

A few of the guys knew I'd been seeing Rachel, although

I hadn't discussed anything about what I knew about her ex. From Rex, I knew it was no secret around town.

I looked out the window, watching the landscape roll by, my eyes bouncing between the trees. The snow was shrinking every day in the shady areas, with very little left. "Of course I'm fine. I might think he's an asshole, but we have a job to do. I'm assuming Rex has backup for whatever the hell is going on with him and his girlfriend."

Beck slowed as he turned onto a side road off the highway. "Yeah, according to Maisie, they've already got the two of them separated. I guess the guy tore the line out right when they arrived."

With anger simmering under the surface, I stayed quiet as we pulled up. Thank God I wasn't working alone.

We swung into motion once we arrived. Maisie had already contacted the local propane company to seal off the line. Beck and I put out the small fire that started in the kitchen as a result. They were damn lucky it was a small tank without much propane in the line.

My frustration, combined with my curiosity, got the best of me when we were finishing up. Rex still had Bruce over by the car. Bruce was cuffed, standing beside one of the deputies, who was jotting something in a small notebook.

Walking past, I heard Bruce say to the deputy who'd just asked him a question, "I wasn't fucking out near Rachel's house again. Am I not allowed to drive out there now?"

Approaching Bruce, I stopped right in front of him. "No, you're not allowed to drive out there."

Bruce sneered. "It's a free country, man. Don't worry, I'll go one night when you're not there."

Anger flashed hot and high inside. I started to step closer, right when I felt a hand curl around my forearm from behind. "Come on, Remy," Beck said. His movement might have looked casual, but his grip on my arm was strong.

Realizing I was standing there with the deputy watching

and Rex across the driveway, talking to the woman I presumed was Bruce's latest girlfriend, I shackled my anger and turned away. I shook my arm free once we rounded behind the car.

"Fucking asshole," I muttered.

"Exactly. He's a fucking asshole and beneath you. Don't waste your time on punching him in front of two cops," Beck countered with a shake of his head. "I get it man, but don't be stupid."

The ride back to the station was quiet. All I could think was I didn't know what the fuck I was going to do when my crew got called to leave town for a few weeks. I wanted Bruce fucking gone.

"How you doing over there?" Beck asked when I leaned my head against the seat with a sigh.

"Fucking pissed. And worried," I added. "He just had to go and make that fucking comment about Rachel's place. There *will* be a night I'm not there. There's not a damn thing I can do about it."

Beck was quiet, his hand resting on the top of the steering wheel as he steered with his wrist. "No, there's not. Seems like this thing with Rachel might be a *thing*, though."

My heart gave a hard *thump*, as if in affirmation. For a beat, I almost laughed. Feelings weren't something I talked about much, but Beck was a good guy and a friend. Much as he teased, he was easy to talk to.

"Yeah, I guess it's a *thing*. Problem is, I'm not so sure how fast she wants things to move. She's pretty skittish. Sounds like she went through hell with Bruce."

Beck rolled to a stop at the intersection to turn onto the main road that ran through downtown Willow Brook. Glancing my way, his gaze was considering. "Yeah, she went through hell. Maisie says that Charlie says that Rachel really likes you. Not that I know much, but the girls usually know everything."

I couldn't help but laugh. "Maybe so, but it doesn't change the fact that she's skittish as hell."

Beck shrugged, looking away as he turned onto the road. "So what? Don't let that stop you. No sense in not making it clear how you feel."

Chapter Twenty-Nine

RACHEL

Setting down my glass of wine, I stared at Remy. "What?"

"I saw Bruce today," Remy repeated.

His expression was controlled, but I sensed the anger simmering under the surface. As safe as I felt with Remy, I knew this was a sore spot for him. Hell, it was a sore spot for me. For damn good reason. Yet, it changed the way I felt when he mentioned Bruce. I didn't want him, or anyone, to think I couldn't handle this shit on my own.

"Where?" My question slipped out. I was honestly curious, but I hated the brief flicker of fear that swamped me. In the time since Bruce had been in my life and I kicked him out of it, I'd learned the fear he created continued to come in waves. There was no rhyme or reason to it.

Sometimes the waves were abrupt and nearly crushing. Other times, they were small and barely knocked me off balance. Over time, they were further and further apart, but they were still there. Just now, I knew I was perfectly safe, with Remy here and Bruce nowhere in sight.

Yet, merely thinking about Bruce churned my stomach and probably always would.

Remy took a quick swig of his beer before answering. "There was a police call out to where he lives with his girlfriend. When they got there, he ripped out the line to the propane tank during the end of their argument, I guess. We got called out to help deal with that."

"Oh," was all I could manage in response.

Remy answered the unspoken question tumbling through my mind. "He was arrested again." Remy looked as if he were considering his next words. "He mentioned you and said it was a free country, so he could drive down your road." His shoulders rose and fell with a deep breath. "I fucking hate that he won't just leave you the hell alone."

That old familiar fear clenched like a fist around my heart. I hated that I knew the feeling so well. While Bruce had been in jail, I knew he was away, so I could control my worries much more easily. I also knew, statistically speaking, I was lucky. Things could've been a lot worse for much longer with him. None of that changed the fact that I felt silly and stupid, and like I should have known better.

I didn't quite know how to deal with how Remy felt about all of it. Having him here was like having my own personal safety blanket, complete with amazing sex.

Yet, I fought hard to handle all this on my own when it was over, to remind myself I could walk forward through life with my head high and take care of myself. Part of me savored Remy's protectiveness, while another part of me wrestled against it. I wanted to lash out. Because I could take care of myself. I had to believe that.

With my emotions a muddled mess inside, I sipped my wine, taking a few deep breaths, and reminding myself all I had to do was just keep moving through to the other side of the fear. I didn't need to make decisions about anything.

"It's not like that's news. Bruce is just trying to get to you. That's the kind of shit he pulls," I finally said, a sense of weariness settling over me. I wondered if I would have to deal with this bullshit from Bruce for the rest of my life.

Remy reached across the counter, catching my hand in his. We were sitting at the stretch of counter between the kitchen and living room, facing each other at an angle. The feel of his thumb brushing back and forth across my wrist was soothing and warm.

"I know that, but..." He was quiet, and then gave his head a small shake. "I don't know the best way to do this. Here's the thing. When everything went down with my sister, she told me afterwards that she hated how everybody protected her from stuff they knew about her ex. I'm trying not to do that. And I know it's personal. But you mean too much to me."

My heart started beating so hard and fast, I could feel the echo of it through my body. I wanted to ask him to clarify just what he meant by that.

Because I knew I was falling in love with him, and I didn't know how to pull back anymore. Having all this bull-shit happen with Bruce right now, just when this was happening with Remy, was downright maddening.

Emotion rushed through me as I scrambled to find purchase inside. "I'm sorry," I heard myself saying, instantly wondering why I was apologizing.

"What the hell are you sorry for? Another thing I know from my sister is this shit just happens. It's random as hell. Maybe I assumed because of how Shay felt that you feel the same way. I would rather let you know about Bruce's comments than keep it to myself and worry about what he might do. If you'd rather me not say anything, just say the word."

Restless, I stood. I was honestly trying to react as reasonably as possible, but I didn't know what I wanted. I didn't want to be shielded, protected. I also didn't want to be stupid. I needed to know Bruce was around and saying bull-shit like that. Yet, I hated how helpless it made me feel, how it made me feel as if he was still dictating the terms of my life, because I had to think about him, to worry about him.

Unsettled, I turned back, my arms wrapped around my waist. "What I want isn't possible. I wish I could undo what happened, so I didn't have to worry about any of this, but I can't. So, no, I don't want you to hide things from me."

Remy was quiet. I felt as if he was trying to read too deeply into my thoughts. Right now, I wasn't quite ready for him to see just how messy I felt inside. Turning away again, I busied myself with washing the dishes.

Henry snapped through the tense moment by trotting to the door and sitting down, as he politely asked to be let outside. By some miracle, I had trained him to go to the door and sit when he needed to go out. There were plenty of things he didn't do, but he did that every time.

"I got him," Remy said as he rose from his stool.

————

The next morning, Remy was called out to a fire. The night before, he slept spooned behind me. As much as I loved being held by him, I couldn't quite relax. I was too unsettled by how quickly I was falling for him. With the intrusion of Bruce back into my world, I didn't know how to deal with Remy's response.

I didn't hold his reaction against him. Not at all. Yet, the whole mess cast shadows of doubt in my mind. What would I do if he weren't here? Like now. I couldn't let myself fall into a situation where I was depending on a man to protect me.

I told myself that it was a good thing he got called out to a fire. It was a little early for a fire this season, but apparently, in an area where they'd had less snowfall than usual, some idiot had decided to start a campfire. With the dry, dead grasses easy fuel, a small fire had kicked up.

Last night had been the first night we slept together and not had sex. I knew exactly why. I was too tense, too tied up in knots, with doubts crowding out all the goodness I felt in the small bubble of time I'd shared with Remy.

On the way into work, I stopped to get gas. My heart stuttered and took off when I looked over and saw the vehicle I now knew to be Bruce's. Of course, he pulled in immediately beside my car, ostensibly to get gas. I knew it was likely he had seen my car and taken the opportunity to play it off as an accidental encounter.

The thing about having a man like Bruce in my past was we didn't even have to actually speak for him to affect me. My body tightened with anxiety, and I felt ready to flee. My breath was shallow and my pulse took off at an unsteady gait.

I breathed through it and got the damn gas. I wasn't going to let him intimidate me. Driving to the office afterwards, I was relieved to throw myself into work.

Charlie and I were checking in at the end of the day, something we did almost every day. She had her feet propped up on one of my chairs, while I got her a cup of tea and myself a cup of coffee.

"So, let me get this straight. You think a little space is good for you and Remy right now?" she asked.

Turning, I handed her a mug of tea. I sank down into a chair at an angle across from her and nodded as I took a sip of my coffee. "Yeah, I do. I think even you have to agree things have been moving a little fast."

"If it was me, I would say that, but it's you. You haven't given any man a chance, not since Bruce."

"All the more reason why I should try to take things slow. Look, I've been able to deal with being alone. I can't just throw myself into this because Remy is all sexy and hot, and makes me feel good and safe," I muttered.

Charlie almost choked on her tea, but managed to swallow it down. Brushing her dark hair away from her forehead and tucking it behind her ear, she took another sip of tea and shook her head. "And what exactly is wrong with all of that? He sounds fucking awesome. Don't get me wrong, I'm totally in love with Jesse..."

I interjected, "Yeah, and you just got married barely over a month ago."

Charlie and Jesse had, in fact, just gotten married. They'd been living together for a year or so, but they recently had a small ceremony after his proposal a few months ago.

Charlie's cheeks flushed, and she smiled softly. "So we did. Anyway, back to my point. I'm totally hot for Jesse, but Remy and that southern accent..." She paused and dramatically put her hand on her chest. "All I've got to say if he's going to be in Willow Brook, I can't deal with him not being with a woman who isn't awesome. He's such a gentleman. He's got that whole sexy, quiet thing going too."

My mind flashed to a few nights ago. He was definitely on the quiet side, and a gentleman. When it came to sex, he was commanding, and I fucking loved it. I vividly remembered the feel of him slapping my ass.

I snapped my mind back to the moment. I did *not* need to be mooning over Remy right now. "Okay, I'll agree with you there." I started to laugh and sobered immediately. "I don't know how to do this. Like, what if this is some weird rebound thing and I'm not really falling for him? Or what if I'm leaning on him too much? I just hate that all this happened right when Bruce got out, and that Bruce had to fucking come back to Willow Brook."

Charlie's gaze was somber as she looked at me. "Yeah, the timing sucks. But maybe it's for the best. I mean, think of it this way. I'd rather see you deal with this bullshit now, than get all comfortable with someone and have it blow up in your face. Whether it's Remy or someone else. As far as I can tell, Remy isn't going anywhere. Jesse told me that he was moody about Bruce around the station the other day. He sounds all protective, which is kind of sweet. You're a badass and bossy as hell, but I wouldn't mind having a man like him around."

I set my coffee down and sighed. I wanted Charlie to be able to tell me what to do, but right now, the doubts were bouncing around in my mind, playing volleyball with my sanity.

I missed Remy. My heart ached for him. When I was home last night, just me and Henry, I wished Remy was there to play fetch with Henry because he could throw farther. That was only one from a long list of wishes. I told myself I didn't miss him that much, but I knew it was a total lie. Alone on the couch, I missed his warmth and resting against his strong chest. I found myself checking the locks on the doors twice and assuring myself Henry would sound the bark alarm if anyone showed up.

Charlie couldn't give me answers, and neither could I.

The following day, Charlie got called to the hospital for an emergency with a patient, so I dropped Em off for her afternoon job. I couldn't resist going into the station. I knew Remy wasn't there, but I also knew Maisie would be able to give me an update on when he might be back.

When I walked into the front area, Lucy was there with Levi, who held little Glory. He had the baby comfortably snuggled in one arm with his other arm thrown around Lucy's shoulders. Looking at them, my heart felt funny. I'd spent the time since Bruce had gone to jail telling myself I probably wouldn't have something like what they had, and now I wanted it so badly, I could taste it. I wanted it with Remy, and I still didn't know how he felt. I still hadn't found clarity in my feelings, and whether they were more of a reaction to Bruce, a rebound, or something else.

Lucy glanced over, casting a smile my way.

"Hey!" Maisie said, looking up from her desk.

"Just dropping Em off, so I thought I'd say hi." Stopping beside Lucy and Levi, I smiled when Glory rolled her head to the side on Levi's shoulder, reaching her hand out, her fingers spread like a star.

Her chubby little fingers curled around mine when I lifted my hand. My heart skipped a few beats.

"So, what brings you by?" I asked, directing my question to Lucy.

"Oh, we have an appointment for Glory with the pediatrician."

"Yep, she's gonna set a weight record." Levi nodded proudly.

Lucy rolled her eyes. "Doubtful. You keep forgetting I'm small. She's totally medium. Not to mention, baby weight isn't a contest."

Levi squeezed Lucy's shoulder. "She's not medium, she's perfect."

That got another eye roll from Lucy. She glanced at the clock above the door behind me. "We need to go, or we'll be late."

"Bye!" Maisie called, while I waved as they turned and left through the front.

My gaze lingered on them through the glass windows as Levi settled Glory into her car seat. Maisie was typing away when I looked back to her.

She'd become a friend over the last few years after she had moved to Willow Brook when she inherited her grandmother's house. "How are Max and Carol?" I asked. "It's been a few weeks since you had card night at your place."

Maisie tapped a button and then pushed the computer keyboard tray back under the counter. "Oh, they're great. Carol's finally mostly sleeping through the night. It took her a lot longer than Max. Every now and then, Beck teases that we should try for another baby, and I'm not so sure. Not that I don't want another baby, I just don't want another whole year where I can hardly sleep," she said with a laugh.

"Rumor has it you forget if you wait long enough," I offered.

Maisie's curls bounced when she giggled. "Right, just like rumor has it that you forget what labor feels like. I have *not* forgotten. Plus, the baby weight is sticking around this time. I told Beck if I have another one, he's gonna have to get used to it."

I rolled my eyes at that. "I'm pretty sure Beck loves every inch of you."

Maisie's cheeks flushed as she shrugged. "Maybe."

I'd known Beck for years. Before he met Maisie, I wouldn't have believed he could settle down. Now, I could hardly remember that he used to be a flirt extraordinaire and a bit of a player. He was still a flirt, but then, Beck was a rather indiscriminate flirt. He would flirt with a chair. But he was downright smitten with Maisie.

"How are things with Remy?" Maisie asked, startling me with a quick shift in conversation.

I stared at her. Remy and I weren't a secret. I'd talked about him with Charlie, and he'd even come up at one of our card nights a few weeks ago now. Somehow, time felt compressed with him. I couldn't believe how little of it had passed since our first kiss.

"I don't know," I finally said. "I mean, they're good, but well, it feels like it's moving pretty quick. I'm worried I'm not thinking too clearly."

"Explain," Maisie said, her wide brown eyes narrowing as she looked at me.

"Just that. After everything that happened with Bruce, well, I'd have been fine if I never got involved with a man ever again. Then, this thing with Remy happened, and now I'm not so sure if it's a rebound, or something more. And Bruce getting out of jail right now and moving back here has totally screwed with my head."

Maisie reached for her water bottle on the desk, taking a quick swig. Setting it down, she regarded me, her gaze considering. "Okay, I get that Bruce showing up would kind of screw with your head. But that would happen no matter what was going on. I mean, right?"

"Well, yeah."

"I don't think this thing with Remy is a rebound. It's been too long since you and Bruce broke up. Just because Remy happens to be the first guy you've gotten involved with doesn't make him a rebound."

I drummed my fingertips on the counter, chewing the corner of my mouth as I considered what she said. "I know, it's not the timing. I just worry. I mean, I need to be able to handle this stuff with Bruce myself. Like, now Remy's out of town and I don't know how long he'll be gone, and I'm all stressed out because Bruce is back in town and I'm at home alone, and..." I paused, taking a deep breath as I felt my words tumbling out wildly. "You get what I'm saying. I just think maybe we need to slow it down, that's all. Plus, I don't even know what Remy wants."

"Remy wants *you*," Macy said with a smile. "That's plain as day. Beck says he talks about you a lot. It's adorable."

The words adorable and Remy in the same sentence made me burst out laughing. Because Remy, well, he was handsome, sexy, and all kinds of tall, dark, and dangerous. But adorable? Not exactly the adjective that came to mind.

Maisie shrugged, laughing along with me. "Just saying." At that moment, the dispatch line rang, and Maisie shifted gears instantly.

I left, only realizing after I was driving away, I forgot to ask her if she had any news on when Remy's crew would be back.

Chapter Thirty

REMY

I set my chainsaw down beside a log and tossed my leather gloves to the ground beside it. Beck glanced at me, running a hand through his shaggy dark curls with a sigh. "Fuck, I'm tired."

He was sitting on the ground, his legs stretched out in front of him, with a water bottle in one hand and a granola bar in the other.

"You and me both, and probably the rest of the crew along with us. This area isn't easy to contain."

We'd been called up to handle a small fire at the start, but stayed in the area to set a controlled burn. The idea was to knock out some of the danger areas and create firebreaks in preparation for summer. Even though we weren't fighting an out-of-control fire, the weather was on our side, and some of the underbrush was damp from the remnants of winter, it was still exhausting work. I loved the work because I could lose myself in it.

I rested my hips on the log and caught the water bottle Beck tossed over from his backpack. "Thanks, man," I murmured quickly before almost draining it.

He flashed a grin and a nod. It had been a long week since we'd flown out here, and we were due to return to Willow Brook tomorrow. Whether I was working or resting, my thoughts meandered down the path Rachel had worn in my brain.

"Ready to get back?" I asked.

"Oh yeah. I miss Maisie and the kids. I still love my job, but being away from them isn't my preference."

"I bet not," I replied.

I still felt slightly unsettled from my last night with Rachel. I held her in my arms as she slept, but I had felt the anxiety running through her and the distance it created between us.

The following afternoon, the tension I'd been holding around my heart eased slightly when I saw Willow Brook come into view from the sky. The helicopter settled down on the landing pad behind the station. In a matter of minutes, we were climbing out, gathering our gear, and walking into the station. All of us were tired and weary.

I watched as Maisie pulled Beck into a hug. I wished Rachel and I were in a place where I knew I could do that. I hated the fact I couldn't help but wonder in the back my mind if Bruce had done anything to stir the pot while I'd been gone.

I texted Rachel before I hopped into the shower, the steaming hot water washing the week away. After I was dressed, I poked my head in Rex's office, figuring he would know if Bruce had done anything in the last week.

Glancing up from his computer screen, he smiled when he saw me, waving me in. "Come on in, Remy."

Slipping into the chair across from his desk, I asked, "Any news?" I figured I didn't need to explain what I meant.

"All is quiet here. Far as I know, Bruce has been laying low at his girlfriend's place."

"You don't think Rachel would blow it off and not let you know if he came around, do you?"

Rex was quiet and then he shrugged. "Maybe. My guess is if it's minor, like him just showing up around town, she's not gonna let me know. But if he shows up at her place again, she'll call."

I drummed my fingertips on the armrest. "I hope I don't come across as... I don't know, like this is more my business than it should be."

Rex shook his head. "Not at all. It's none of my business what's going on with you and Rachel, but as far as I'm concerned, we take care of each other around here. I'm glad Rachel has you."

At that moment, my phone buzzed in my pocket just as Rex's desk phone rang. "I gotta take this," he said as he glanced over to the phone.

"Gotcha. Thanks for giving me a few minutes," I replied as I stood to leave his office. Sliding my phone out of my pocket, I glanced down to see Rachel had responded to my text.

I'm actually busy tonight. It's card night with my friends. Rain check?

———

Four fucking days had passed, and I still hadn't seen Rachel since I got back. Frustration was simmering inside me all the damn time now.

I knew pressuring Rachel wasn't likely to help matters, yet I was impatient. Hell, I was more than impatient. I missed her in more ways than one. I didn't like feeling as if she had shut me out. She hadn't completely ignored me. She responded to my texts, each time with an excuse of why she was tied up and busy.

What was bothering me now was she hadn't answered my last two texts. I was worried and getting more concerned by the minute. I was curbing the urge to drive by and check on her, if only because I didn't want to behave the same way Bruce did. I didn't own her.

It was late evening after work, and I found myself pulling into the parking lot at Firehouse Café. I wasn't up for the crowd at Wildlands. The cool spring evening air gusted in with me when I pushed open the door. It was quieter than it was in the mornings, with a few couples at tables, but no line. Janet glanced up, her smile widening when she saw me.

"Hey Remy!"

Stopping at the counter, I rested my hip against it and tried to smile, but it was an effort. "Hey, Janet, how's it going?"

She cocked her head to the side. "Something's off, but first, you need coffee. The usual house coffee?"

"Sounds good."

Janet spun away, quickly snagging one of the distinctive red cups and filling it. She added my preferred dash of cream without even asking and turned back, sliding it across the counter to me. I tossed a five-dollar bill on the counter. "Keep the change."

Taking a sip, I closed my eyes and sighed. "You make damn good coffee, Janet."

She was grinning when I opened my eyes again. "I get plenty of practice. Now tell me why you look a little..." She paused, pursing her lips. "Tense?"

Janet had this way of making people talk to her, probably because even though she knew practically everyone and everything, she was bone-deep good and didn't throw gossip around. Although she probably knew more gossip than anyone else in Willow Brook.

"I think Rachel's avoiding me," I finally said.

While I certainly hadn't given Janet the blow-by-blow, seeing as Rachel and I had stopped here for coffee together more than once, it wasn't as if Janet had no clue we had something going on. Janet twisted her lips and let out a sigh. "Is she?"

"Maybe. All I know is I haven't seen her since before I left, over a week and a half ago now."

"Go see her," Janet said.

"Are you sure that's a good idea? I don't..."

"I know you don't want to seem like her ex, but you're nothing like him. She needs to know you care because she isn't likely to believe it without it being so obvious she can't ignore it."

I eyed Janet and shrugged. "I'm not so sure."

"Well, being not so sure isn't exactly the way to declare your feelings," Janet said flatly, just as the bell above the door jingled behind me.

Turning, I saw a couple with two small children entering. Looking to Janet, I lifted my coffee cup in thanks. "I'll think on it. Always good to see you."

Janet winked. "Of course. Don't think too hard."

With Janet's words ringing in my mind, I found myself pulling out and heading in Rachel's direction. My place was in the opposite direction of town. Truth be told, ever since I'd spent those two weeks with Rachel, my home felt cavernous and empty.

I actually liked my house. I'd snapped it up from a couple who had decided to move back to the lower forty-eight, after they had a baby and wanted to be closer to family. It was a lucky buy for me, and nestled amongst some trees. There was even a small pond on the property off to the side of the house, with a winding path through the trees leading to it. With a larger lake nearby feeding into the pond through a connecting stream, fishing for lake trout was an option.

Usually, when I was feeling restless, I went home and walked to the pond because I loved fishing. It was a quiet, peaceful activity. Right now though, that held no appeal. I found peace hard to come by in the echoing silence from Rachel.

I pulled off the side of the road, thinking I should call her first. The phone rang several times and then she answered. Her voice sounded god-awful. She coughed in the middle of saying hello.

"You okay?" I asked, concern swiftly replacing the frustration I'd been feeling.

A hacking cough was her answer, loud enough I had to pull the phone away from my ear. "I'm sick," she finally muttered when she stopped coughing.

"I'll be right there."

I didn't wait for her reply, and the line went dead in my ear. Reaching her house in minutes, I was relieved when the door opened as I turned the knob, concern following instantly. If I could walk right in, so could Bruce. But that was something to worry about at another time.

Henry greeted me, circling my legs quickly. Glancing across the room, I saw Rachel stretched out on the couch. She had two blankets piled on top of her. From across the room, I could see the fevered flush on her skin. I strode quickly to her. In the minutes since we'd been on the phone, she'd fallen asleep.

My heart squeezed, worry spinning inside. Just as I was debating whether or not to wake her, her eyes flickered open, her gaze glassy and tired. "Oh, I didn't know you were coming over," she mumbled.

I held a hand to her forehead. She was burning up. "Have you taken anything for that fever?" I asked softly.

Henry joined me at the edge of the couch, pressing the entire side of his body against it and angling his head across her thigh. His tail thumped against the cushion.

"I took some Ibuprofen, but it's been a few hours. You didn't have to come over," she said as she tried to sit up before collapsing back into the couch.

"I'm not going anywhere. When's last time you had something to eat or drink?"

"I don't know," she said, sounding defeated.

Her lips were dry and cracked. Giving a quick squeeze along her forearm, I rose and walked back across the room.

After hanging up my jacket, I checked the thermostat by the door, realizing she probably hadn't even noticed the heat was low.

After turning it up, I investigated in the kitchen. My mama had insisted I learn to cook, so I was pretty handy around the kitchen. I figured I could at least whip up some chicken soup.

I managed to find a package of chicken breasts in the freezer, along with some onions and garlic. After making some tea and carrying it over to the couch, I fetched two Ibuprofen from the bathroom and helped prop her up on some pillows. She managed to take a few sips and swallow down the pills. I hoped they would help with the fever.

"You okay if I take Henry out for a little bit?" I asked when she appeared conscious enough to answer.

She nodded. "Please do. I'm sure he's feeling stir-crazy. This knocked me out yesterday and it's just worse today."

I hated seeing her like this. Leaning forward, I pressed a kiss to her forehead before straightening again. Henry had heard his name and was spinning excitedly around my feet.

"You want the TV on?"

She carefully took another sip of tea, gripping the mug tightly in her hands. "Might as well."

Her breath had a little rattle to it as I turned away. I found the remote on the floor and turned the TV on before handing it to her. I knew she enjoyed watching the house repair shows and cooking shows, so I selected one of the cooking channels. I figured if she stayed awake, she could pick whatever she wanted.

"Come on, buddy," I said to Henry as I strolled across the living room and slipped my boots back on.

Once we were outside, all I did was stand in one place and throw the ball over and over and over again for Henry. He was near crazed with energy once we were out there, running like a wild dog, his tongue flapping as he raced back to me every time.

His pattern was to fetch for a little bit and then pause to take a bathroom break in the trees. He instantly returned to me, dropping the ball at my feet, and we set off on another round of fetch. When he finally started to slow and tire, I took him inside and fed him dinner. Rachel's eyes opened when we came in, and she lifted her fingers in a wave. Otherwise, she barely moved.

After Henry had dinner, I got to work. I chopped up the onions and garlic and sautéed them as I thawed the chicken in some hot water. I could whip up a batch of chicken stew and dumplings easily. Beyond the onions and garlic, there weren't many vegetables to choose from, so I went with a bag of mixed frozen vegetables in the freezer. After I seasoned the stew with tarragon, pepper, and a dash of salt, I made dumplings and let them simmer on the top.

I heard something resembling a croak from the living room and glanced over to see Rachel trying to get off the couch.

"Don't move," I called over. "I'm bringing you a bowl of soup."

"I have to pee," she muttered with a laugh that turned into a hacking cough.

After turning the burner off under the soup, I walked over. She made it halfway across the room, but paused when she started coughing again.

"Have you called Charlie?" I asked as I steadied her with an arm around her waist.

"She knows I'm sick because I called out of work. It's just a cold," Rachel managed, in between harsh coughs.

"Maybe so, but it sounds pretty bad."

"I'm not taking antibiotics. Plus, Charlie won't give them to me anyway. They've been way overprescribed. The best thing for a cold is rest and fluids," she said on the heels of a ragged breath.

"I wasn't suggesting you take antibiotics. Just thinking maybe somebody should take a look."

She straightened and took a few more steps. I decided I didn't give a damn if it pissed her off. I was helping her walk to the bathroom. It was clear she was weak and unsteady on her feet.

After we got through the door, she looked up at me. "You're not staying to watch me pee," she announced with a lift of her chin.

I chuckled, relieved to see her attitude assert itself. "Wasn't planning on it, but I'll be right outside the door."

With a roll of her eyes, she shuffled past me. I stepped out, pulling the door shut and leaning against the wall nearby. Henry lifted his head from where he had settled in on his favorite chair beside the couch, and I could see the concern in his eyes. I didn't give a damn if some people thought it was crazy, but I knew dogs could sense things. It was clear Henry was aware his human wasn't feeling too good.

After a few minutes, I heard the toilet flush and water running in the sink. The door opened, and Rachel stood there, looking as if the exertion of walking to the bathroom had wiped her out all over again. The underlying feverish tint was bright on her pale skin. I hoped her fever would start to go down soon.

She didn't resist my help with walking back across the room. After I got her situated on the couch, making sure the pillows propped her up and the blankets were tucked around her legs, I straightened.

"I don't know what you made, but it smells really good. That's saying something because I can't smell much," she said, her voice raspy and tired.

I grinned and pressed a kiss to her forehead. "Chicken stew with dumplings. It's coming right up."

She pointed me to a folding tray, which I set up beside her. After I delivered a bowl of soup to her, along with more tea, I filled a bowl for myself and joined her on the couch.

"Oh my God," she mumbled, between bites, "This is

amazing. I wish my taste buds were working a little better because it's delicious, and I can't even really taste it."

"Good. You need to get something in you."

After she ate, she leaned back into the pillows with a sigh, her eyes closing. I returned to the kitchen, washed the dishes, and put everything away. I had made enough soup to last her for a few more days. Her eyes opened again when I sat down on the couch beside her.

"You're going to get sick if you stay," she said before she began coughing harshly again.

"I'm not going anywhere, sweetheart. If I'm gonna get sick, I'll get sick, but I'm not leaving you alone like this. Plus, Henry needs someone to walk him."

I tacked that last bit on because I figured she would worry more about Henry than herself.

A rattling sigh escaped. "You're right. Thanks for taking him out."

She drifted into sleep while the television rumbled low in the background. Meanwhile, I wasn't going anywhere until she felt better.

Chapter Thirty-One

RACHEL

At some point during the night, I awoke, my own cough jolting me out of sleep. For a moment, I was disoriented. Then, I realized I was burrowed against Remy's chest with the blankets tucked over both of us. Before he arrived last night, I'd been having those awful feverish shivers where I couldn't quite get the heat to seep through my body, even though I was hot from the fever.

Held fast against him, his body a bulwark of strength and heat, I was finally warm all the way through. The worst of the feverish feeling had passed, although I knew that was likely due to the Ibuprofen. I could still feel the fever under the surface, waiting to break through.

I was so tired and so weak. I hated needing someone, but I was relieved Remy had shown up last night. Lifting my head carefully, I glanced around the room. A light had been left on in the bathroom, likely on purpose, imparting a soft glow into the living room. Henry was sound asleep on his favorite chair. The television was off, and the house was quiet.

Another cough rose up, taking over this time. In a matter

of seconds, I was coughing, harsh and deep, barely able to catch my breath. I could feel Remy come awake from the slight tension in his body. "Let me get you some cough medicine."

I shook my head in between coughs. "Don't want you to move," I finally said, feeling vulnerable for even saying it aloud, but too sick to care.

"I'll be right back." His hands gently eased me to his side. He slid out from under me and returned a moment later, handing me a small plastic cup filled with a dose of cough medicine. I gulped it down.

"That stuff tastes so yucky," I rasped.

Remy immediately swapped the empty medicine cup with a glass of water. I sipped it gratefully, chasing away the medicinal flavor in my throat.

"Sure does, but it'll help with that cough."

Just like he said, Remy returned to the couch, pulling me back onto his strong chest and tucking the blankets around us. After a few more coughs, I settled against him with a sigh. "Aren't you hot?" I murmured into his chest.

"Don't worry about me, sweetheart."

I savored the rumble of his voice against my ear, drifting into sleep and thinking I could get used to this.

Almost a week later, I sat on my couch, absently watching a cooking show. Remy had left because he actually had to work. I had called in to try to persuade the office to let me come in, but Charlie and Doc were adamant I needed to wait until my cough was gone.

They had ignored my argument that I was past the point of contagion. Remy had been gone a mere two days, and I started missing him about an hour after he left. Although I'd been half out of it, it hadn't slipped my attention that he took damn good care of me when I was at my worst.

Obviously, I would've survived without him, but his chicken stew and dumplings had been manna from heaven. His insistence on keeping me supplied with hot tea and checking my fever made my heart ache just thinking about it.

I finally had enough strength to shower last night. After that, I felt close to human. There was nothing left beyond a lingering cough and a little congestion.

Meanwhile, I had no idea what to do. Remy had left for Fairbanks for some training and was scheduled to be gone for three days. He offered to cancel, and yet, I couldn't let him do that. Although I had wanted to. Badly.

He had been gone for two nights and texted several times a day. I missed him, and I was all a muddle inside. In a little bit, I was leaving to go over for card night at Holly's place. We used to go to her apartment, but now she was all moved in with Nate. Holly was yet another one of my friends who was madly in love.

I was thrilled for her. It just made me wish I could see a little more clearly when it came to my own love life. With a mental shake, I stood and padded into my bedroom. After a quick shower, I changed into actual clothes.

As I reached my door, my hand pressing lightly on the knob, I glanced back to Henry. "You be a good boy, okay?"

His tail thumped, but in a flash, his entire demeanor shifted. His ears perked up, and he lifted his head, the hair on the back of his neck rising slightly. A sense of fear skated through me, that cold feeling balling in my stomach.

When I glanced outside, I saw a moose ambling across the road into the driveway. I relaxed instantly. I could deal with a moose.

Henry trotted over to the front window, his nose barely clearing the sill as he watched the moose disappear into the trees on the far side of the drive. Stepping away from the door, I walked to Henry, scrubbing behind his ears with my fingers. His tail thumped against my legs as I turned away.

A moose or Bruce, Henry always let me know when someone showed up.

Holly and Nate lived on the other side of Willow Brook from me. As I drove through town, I stopped by the grocery store to pick up a bottle of wine and some chips. I was standing in the aisle, scanning the selection, when a prickle of awareness raced up my spine. Without even turning around, I knew Bruce was here. That old fear was there, but strangely, a sense of calm anger followed.

Turning, I found him standing perhaps ten feet away. He wasn't looking at me, but I didn't doubt for a second, he knew I was right here. I took a few steps in his direction. "Bruce, cut the shit," I said flatly.

He looked up, and I took the moment to observe him. His brown hair was cropped close to his head, and his blue eyes stood out. He was a fit man, and I hated thinking about how he used his strength.

No matter what, he was handsome. I now knew the way I felt when we were first together had been a reaction to nothing more than superficial charm. The initial burst of attraction burned up into ashes and dust when the veneer wore thin.

"I don't know what the hell you're talking about, Rachel. If you call the fucking police on me for being at the grocery store, well, that's a bunch of bullshit," he muttered, his gaze flat.

I could feel a familiar vibe in him, the anticipation of my reaction. I knew he was waiting to feed off it. Even though cold fear had knotted in my stomach, I didn't react. There was nothing left. He was a petty, violent man, but I wasn't going to allow him to have a hold on me anymore.

A couple turned down into the aisle behind him, talking about something. Meanwhile, at my back, I could hear a mother and her teenage son debating the finer points of which snacks he wanted. I knew the grocery store was filled with people. No matter what had passed between Bruce and me before, I was safe here. That knowledge emboldened me.

"It's not my responsibility to avoid you. It's your responsibility to avoid me. If you think, for a second, that by hanging around town, you can get to me, you can't."

Bruce's eyes narrowed. I could feel him sizing me up and almost felt a slight tinge of surprise from him. I took a slow breath, mentally squaring my shoulders and clinging to the strength I had regained since he'd hurt me.

"I suggest you get the hell out of town. Leave your girlfriend behind and let her have some peace. Willow Brook is small. You won't be able to shake your history here," I said.

Bruce was quiet and then he finally muttered something under his breath.

"Excuse me?" I countered.

"Fuck off, Rachel."

He turned and walked away. I didn't know how, but somehow, I knew he wouldn't bother me again. His power and control manipulation relied on someone feeling weak. Although I was still piecing my life back together and would always carry scars from what happened, Bruce's hold on me was over.

I couldn't erase the past and how I had stumbled into that mess, but I could shake free of the effect he had on me.

———

"Dammit!" Lucy exclaimed as she tossed the remaining cards in her hand on the table, casting a barely good-natured glare in Maisie's direction.

"We know. You hate losing," Amelia offered dryly.

"You just won the last hand," Maisie added.

Lucy rolled her eyes. As noted, Lucy hated losing. Maisie was damn good at cards and usually won. Funny thing was, when Lucy did beat Maisie, she was always suspicious Maisie threw the game just to let her win.

We were sitting on stools surrounding the kitchen island at Holly and Nate's house. Between rounds of cards, we nibbled on snacks and sipped drinks. And talked. There was always plenty of talking. Or rather, gossip.

With a grin, Holly set down a fresh bowl of guacamole before slipping her hips onto the stool beside me. "I won tonight too," she said with a wink.

Lucy shrugged, already letting go of her most recent loss.

"So, tell us, how are things with Remy?" Holly asked, completely startling me with her abrupt shift in topic.

I had conveniently just dipped a tortilla chip into the guacamole and bought myself a minute while I chewed. I was under no illusions that my friends might have been wondering. Within our tight circle, we generally didn't consider it gossip to wonder what was up with each other's love lives, or lack thereof.

Charlie was across from me and caught my eye, a hint of a gleam in hers. She knew Remy had nursed me those days when I was so sick. She also pointed out that perhaps I should let Remy know how I felt because I was worrying too much.

Looking to Holly, I shrugged. "Things are good. He's due back in another day. The last time I saw him, I was sick, so..." My words trailed off.

Charlie filled in that blank, quite helpfully. "Remy went over and took care of you, made you chicken soup, and called me and made me come over to check to see if your fever was too high."

Amelia's brows hitched. "Oh my. That—"

"Sounds serious," Lucy interjected.

"I heard the same thing. That's why I was wondering how things were going. I think Remy's serious about you, and you'd be stupid not to jump all over that. Back when I was in denial about Nate, I tried to think Remy was hot. I couldn't get it to be anything other than superficial. I mean, he *is* hot, but not that way for me," Holly explained, her brown eyes knowing as she looked at me.

"Oh my God. How often have you all been talking about this?"

"Probably as much as you all talked about me and Nate," Holly offered with a shrug.

Lucy snorted. "I know how much I hate when people gossip, but we don't count."

"It's not gossip if we care, and we need to make sure she ends up with sexy-as-hell Remy," Amelia added.

I looked around the table at my well-meaning, nosy friends, and sighed. "I'm getting up the nerve. I wasn't exactly up for it when I was coughing and hacking and had a fever. Plus, who knows what he wants?"

"Oh, he wants you," Maisie said as she returned from the bathroom, clearly not missing any of the conversation.

"But, how do you know?" I asked.

"Because I see the way he looks at you. Get over yourself," she said firmly as she slipped back onto a stool and grabbed a tortilla chip.

Looking amongst my friends, I kept my next sigh to myself. Though my passing interaction with Bruce on the way here had somehow helped me see I was finally past a certain part of what he did to me, I was still struggling with just how much I wanted to lean on Remy.

I didn't quite feel like having that conversation in a group. So, I rolled my eyes and assured my friends of the obvious. "Of course I know Remy's sexy as hell, and a good catch. Plus, the man can cook. The chicken and dumplings he made me were amazing, even though I could hardly taste."

If they knew I was avoiding the deeper part of the topic, my friends loved me enough to let it slide.

Chapter Thirty-Two

RACHEL

The next day, I was anxious to get a text from Remy and kept obsessively checking my phone while I was at the office. The last few times he'd been gone for work, he texted when he got back.

When I heard nothing, those old doubts, strong and opinionated, started to kick up a fuss in my brain, reminding me why someone as awesome as Remy might not want things to get too serious with me. Maybe it was just sex, maybe he was just being nice when he happened to call when I was sick.

Under the surface of that was the quieter voice, the voice that was often drowned out by my shrill, doubting critic. That voice tried to remind me of how things felt when we were together—the intensity, the intimacy, that ethereal connection. It transcended any physical qualities.

After finally getting clearance to return to work, I had more than enough to do to catch up, so at least I had that to keep me from constantly checking my phone. When I finished up for the day, I had to hunt around the office for my cell phone. Occasionally, I left it in examining rooms as I rushed from one patient to the next. I found it on the counter beside the computer in the charting room where I had left it plugged in to charge when the battery got low.

With a muttered curse, I snatched it up. I hoped upon hope that a text from Remy would be waiting for me.

Instead, there was a text from Maisie, along with three missed calls from her personal cell phone.

Where the hell are you? I'm trying to let you know that Remy is really sick, and they took him to the hospital when he got back.

I tapped the call back button as I hurried down the hallway at the office. Maisie picked up right away.

"What the hell is going on with Remy? I'm on my way over right now."

"I guess it started out as a cough, and he kept working. Because, you know, men are idiots. According to Beck, this morning, his fever spiked. They were already due to fly back, so that's what they did. Remy's not too happy about them insisting he get cleared at the hospital, but that's where he is," Maisie explained.

"Have you heard anything since they took him over there?" I asked as I grabbed my coat from the back of my office chair and hurried out.

"No, just that he's there for an evaluation. Beck promised me he would call as soon as he had an update."

"I bet he caught whatever I had. I feel awful," I said, scrambling into my car.

"You had a cold. Even if he got your cold, it's not your fault he got that sick," Maisie said calmly. "I gotta go. Just got a call on the dispatch line."

"Thanks for..." I didn't get to finish as the line went dead in my ear.

I didn't take it personally, seeing as she was responsible for handling emergency calls. I zipped over to the hospital, probably breaking every speeding law on the way over and grateful I might be able to sweet talk Rex out of giving me a ticket if I happened to get pulled over.

Moments later, I hurried in through the main entrance at the hospital, looking around wildly. The ER here had two tracks—the cases for blatant emergencies, such as a severe injury, and then the cases like Remy's, where the emergency level was a little lower. Hurrying down the hallway, I aimed toward the wing where I thought he should be.

Charlie happened to be here for an afternoon rotation. I caught sight of her dark ponytail swinging and called her name. She turned back and waved.

"Have you seen Remy?" I asked, not even bothering with a hello when I reached her.

Charlie gaze softened. "I was just about to call you. He's going to be fine, but we're admitting him. He's got viral pneumonia."

"Oh my God, where is he?"

She pointed over her shoulder with her thumb to the room she had just exited. "I just found out he was here, or I'd have called you sooner. He's in there and none too pleased with my recommendation. My guess is, it started with a cold. There are more than enough viruses bouncing around town. Like an idiotic man, he went right out into the field, where it's cold and damp, and worked his ass off."

I started to brush past her, and she caught me at the elbow. "He's exhausted." I stared at her, tears hot in my eyes and my throat tightening with emotion. "Are you okay?" she asked, her voice softening.

I nodded quickly, trying to take a breath through the thickness in my throat. "I'm fine. I don't know why I'm freaking out," I murmured with a shaky sigh.

"He just needs rest, medication, and some fluids."

I stared at her, nodding jerkily. She didn't say anything, just let her hand slide up to my shoulder to give it a squeeze. "He's going to be fine. Go in and see him. It's not likely anyone here will enforce visiting hours, not with you," she said with a soft smile.

Just then, her name was called over the pager system.

With another squeeze on my shoulder, she hurried off. Opening the door to Remy's hospital room, I closed it behind me quietly after I stepped through. He was under the covers, his eyes closed. With my heart still tight, I approached the bed. When I stopped beside it, his eyes opened and he rolled his head to the side. He looked like hell. His skin had a flushed, feverish tone, and his eyes were glassy. He looked utterly exhausted.

My man, my strong Remy, was completely wiped out.

"Hey," I said softly. Laying my hand carefully on his forearm where it rested on the mattress, I lifted the other to brush his hair away from his forehead. "Looks like I gave you that cold after all."

Remy's lips quirked. "Don't know. Maybe, but two of the guys on the crew have that same nasty cold. Charlie just gave me a lecture..." He stopped, a harsh cough cutting into his words.

I glanced around, my eyes landing on a small plastic cup of water on the tray beside his bed. I added more water from the pitcher beside it and handed it to him when he finally managed to stop hacking. He took several sips and then leaned back, even more weary after that bout of coughing.

My heart squeezed. "So, what did Charlie say?" I asked when he finally seemed to be breathing normally again.

"Said I shouldn't have worked so hard. She thinks between the weather and pushing it too hard, I've got viral pneumonia. Whatever the hell that is. She wants to keep me overnight and I do *not* want to be here."

"Yeah, she mentioned that on my way in." I brushed his hair away from his forehead again, feeling a clench of worry at the feverish heat from his skin. "Charlie's not one to over-react, so if she says you need to stay for tonight, then you need to stay."

Remy collapsed against the pillows with a sigh, the sound rattling slightly in his lungs. "Right. Says you who wouldn't even see the doctor when you were sick."

"Do you want some tea?" I asked, ignoring his slight jab.

"What I want is to be home. I don't need you nursing me, along with the nurses here," he mumbled.

I narrowed my eyes. "I'm not going anywhere. You didn't answer me about the tea."

He set the plastic cup down on the tray and nodded. "It'll probably feel better on my throat."

As I turned to step away from the bed, he caught my hand in his. Looking back, my breath hitched in my throat. Even though he was sick, clearly exhausted, and probably miserable, somehow, this man managed to give me one of those sexy looks, one where I felt like his eyes were searing my skin.

"I missed you," he said softly, and then promptly lapsed into another bout of coughing.

When he was done, I filled the cup again and handed it to him. All the while, my heart tumbled in funny little beats in my chest. "I missed you too."

He held my gaze, the look there so intense, it stole my breath. Then, he started coughing again.

"I'm going to get you some tea, and find out if Charlie can get you something for that cough," I said, the next time his cough lapsed.

Chapter Thirty-Three

REMY

A full two weeks later, I was resting on the couch at my house with Henry curled up at my feet and Rachel busy in the kitchen. Apparently, pneumonia sucked. Or so I learned. Probably because I was the worst patient she ever had, Charlie reluctantly discharged me from the hospital after one night. She wanted me to have enough fluids and something to take the edge off my cough.

She ordered me to rest at home, rather sternly. I hadn't meant to do so. In fact, I had assumed I would maybe take a few days off until I got my energy back, and then go back to work. That wasn't quite how it worked out. It was a good week before I felt like I had enough energy to do much of anything, other than sleep and wake up long enough to eat and snuggle on the couch with Rachel.

Rachel had insisted on taking me home from the hospital. My recovery time had started at her place, but we ended up decamping to my place after the first night. Of course, I told her Henry could come, and it was more comfortable. She finally admitted she'd been meaning to sell her house anyway because it had too many memories of Bruce.

I didn't really know because I hadn't had the energy to investigate, but I assumed she'd pretty much reorganized my entire kitchen. While I could certainly cook and was better than average, I couldn't have cared less how my kitchen was organized. Rachel, on the other hand, had all kinds of opinions about what should go where. In the first few days, she had asked tons of questions about where to find things, occasionally slipping up with a grumble about it. I'd given her free rein to do whatever she wanted.

"How are you doing over there?" she called as she adjusted the heat under a large stainless-steel pot.

"Just fine, sweetheart, just fine. Whatcha making?"

"More chicken and dumplings," she replied.

I discovered she could make a divine batch of chicken and dumplings. She'd been switching it up, but pretty much forcing me to subsist on soup ever since I got out of the hospital.

Not that I was complaining. At all. The woman could cook. I was pretty sure she could make boiled water taste amazing at this point.

"I also made fresh bread while you were napping," she added.

"Is that what smells so good?" I gave Henry a stroke on his head and rose from the couch, striding into the kitchen to investigate.

I had only felt well enough to stand for more than a few minutes at a time over the last few days. When I stepped into the kitchen area, the scent of fresh bread assailed me.

"It smells like heaven," I murmured as I stepped behind Rachel, slipping my arms around her waist and leaning down to dust a few kisses along the side of her neck.

It had been too damn long since we had sex. Just now, with her lush bottom pressed against me, my body immediately responded, my cock thickening and lengthening in a matter of seconds.

"You smell even better," I added, brushing a few more kisses along her neck and nipping at her earlobe.

She giggled. "Behave," she ordered. "You're not one hundred percent yet."

Reaching around her, I turned off the burner and removed the ladle from her hand, setting it on the counter beside the stove.

"I don't have to be one hundred percent, sweetheart."

"Remy, you..." Her words trailed off as I turned her in my arms and palmed her ass, rocking my arousal into the cradle of her hips. Her cheeks flushed and her mouth fell open in a lovely little O.

"What was that you were saying?"

Her hair was in a loose ponytail with tendrils falling around her face. She wore a pair of sweatpants that hung low on her hips and a long sleeve T-shirt. I supposed few would consider her outfit sexy. Except me.

I slid my hand under her shirt, almost groaning at the feel of her silky skin as I dragged my palm up over her belly to cup one of her breasts. Her nipple was taut through the silk of her bra when I pinched it with my thumb and forefinger. I rocked my hips into her again.

"You didn't answer," I teased.

A little moan escaped before she answered. "You're not all better yet."

"I feel quite fine. In fact, I feel better already."

She gasped when I flicked the clasp between her breasts, a low growl escaping at the feel of her warm skin and the heavy weight of her breast in my palm.

"You need to eat," she murmured, a whimper following when I dipped my head, grazing my teeth lightly along the soft skin on her neck.

I'd come to learn her body well—all the little places that made her crazy. A sweet spot low on the side of her neck was one of them, and her nipples were crazy sensitive.

"We'll eat in a little bit," I murmured, finally catching her lips in a kiss. She sighed, the warm sweetness of her mouth welcoming me in, her tongue darting out and slicking against mine.

Perfect.

Need lashed at me, and I was suddenly feeling almost frantic for more. Perhaps it was because it had been so long. I'd never thought a few weeks would feel like an eternity, but when it came to being intimate with Rachel, it was too damn long.

Stepping back slightly, I slipped her sweatpants down over her hips, her panties right along with them. Rachel cried out when I reached between her thighs to find her hot and ready, her pussy slick with her arousal.

I needed her naked because I needed to see all of her. With a rough tug, I tossed her shirt aside. She stood before me, my eyes tracking over her plump breasts, and the flare of her hips. She shifted her legs, the subtle sound of moisture heightening the need twisting inside me. I teased my fingers in her arousal.

Bending low, I dragged my tongue around a nipple, sucking it lightly as she cried out. I might not have been one hundred percent, as Rachel worried, but I had no trouble lifting her on the counter and pushing her knees apart. Glancing down, the sight of her pink, swollen, and glistening pussy greeted me.

With a few kisses on the inside of her thighs, her body rippled. I wanted to take it slow, but I needed her too much. I buried my face between her thighs, savoring the salty tang, her musky scent washing over me. When I buried two fingers in her channel and sucked lightly on her clit, she came in a rough, noisy burst.

She was freeing my cock from my jeans before I had fully straightened. Her legs curled around my hips and she rocked forward as I surged into her snug, wet core. I almost came instantly. I had to force myself to hold still, my forehead falling to hers.

She giggled. "Well, I guess you are feeling better."

"Told you," I said gruffly. We held still like that for a few beats. I could feel the flutter of her pulse where her breasts pressed against my chest. Emotion rocked me.

"In case you haven't figured it out yet, I love you."

Rachel was quiet, her breath coming in soft pants. I didn't care if she was ready, she needed to know how I felt. After a moment, she murmured, "Look at me."

Lifting my head, I found her blue gaze waiting, vulnerability and emotion shining there. "I can't say that I figured that out yet, but I figured out that *I* love *you.*"

I caught her lips in a kiss, drawing back slowly and sinking inside of her core again. What had started as a rushed, frantic need for release spiraled into a slow and sensuous lovemaking on the kitchen counter.

With her legs curled around my hips as I rocked into her, every breath and every heartbeat echoed her name.

My release was intense, building inside, pressure gathering like a wave, and then hot, sizzling electricity bundling at the base of my spine and shooting upward through me. Rachel's cry was right ahead of mine, my name a rough shout as her sex clenched and rippled around my cock, drawing my release out.

Afterwards, she looked over at me and laughed softly. "How did it end up that I'm completely naked and you still have all your clothes on?"

I shrugged. "I guess I was in a hurry."

After we untangled ourselves, she tugged her clothes back on and joined me on the couch for soup and fresh bread. I fell asleep later, with her warm against my side, thinking I was the luckiest man in the world.

Chapter Thirty-Four

RACHEL

Pushing through the door into Firehouse Café, I found it a little crowded. Although the air was still cool in the mornings, the tourists were starting to crowd the small towns of Alaska. It was still technically spring and not even summer here yet, but so what? Once the snow was gone and the roads were clear, out-of-state visitors crowded the usually sparsely traveled highways of Alaska.

Due to its proximity to Anchorage and the pristine coast nearby, Willow Brook often saw some of the earliest tourists. I stepped to the back of the line and glanced around. There were a few familiar faces mixed in, but the balance was definitely starting to shift.

I was here on a coffee run from the office at lunch and had a list of sandwiches to pick up as well. Janet caught my eye from behind the counter and winked. Her attention shifted away quickly as she handed over someone's coffee and rang them up.

"Hey," a voice said from behind me. Glancing back, I found Maisie standing there, brushing her curls out of her eyes.

"Hey, lunch run?" I asked.

"For me and Rex. He forgot to bring the lunch Georgie made for him this morning, so he called me on my way into the station. Em is working today since it's an in-service day at school, so we've got her doing training duty on the dispatch line. With Rex there for backup, she can handle it."

The bell jingled again. When I looked back, my pulse kicked up a notch when I saw Remy walking in. The moment his eyes landed on me, my heart did a little happy dance, and heat radiated from my core, spinning through my body.

Maisie glanced back, a grin stretching across her face. "Hey, Remy, are you on coffee duty for the guys?"

He smiled, nodding as he stepped to my side. Bending low, he pressed a kiss to my lips, then slipped his arm around my waist, tugging me right up to his side. It had been a month since his bout of pneumonia, and I'd all but moved in with him at this point.

He'd insisted on helping me move my clothes and everything I wanted from my kitchen last weekend, declaring it was silly for me to be running home every other day.

"Hey," I said, glancing up into his warm gaze. Butterflies spun in my belly at the look in his eyes.

"Hey," he replied. "What are you doing here?"

"Getting lunch and coffee for everybody at the office."

"No need to answer me," Maisie teased.

Remy glanced over and grinned. "Sorry 'bout that. Yup, I'm on coffee duty for the guys."

"Next time, call me first," Maisie replied with a grin.

Remy's hand was resting on my hip, and he gave it a squeeze. In the time since I stopped fighting how I felt about him, I'd come to learn Remy was all about affection all the time. He bordered on possessive, and I didn't mind it, not one bit. Remy didn't carry the underlying jealousy and greed Bruce had exhibited, that had left me feeling so unsettled. With Remy, it was all about just being wrapped up in the heartbeat of intimacy that pounded between us.

He dipped his head again, pressing a kiss to my cheek and then to each corner of my mouth. Sweet hell, those corner kisses just melted me. It didn't matter that we were in the middle of Firehouse Café, surrounded by people with one of my closest friends standing nearby. I lost sight of everything but Remy.

Maisie's laugh broke into my awareness. "Hey, line's moving. You're holding people up now."

Looking ahead, I saw there was a gap between me and Remy and the rest of the line, not to mention that a few other customers had come in behind him. My cheeks felt hot, but I shrugged, stepping forward with Maisie following.

"You two are ridiculous," she stated with a grin.

Remy didn't even bother to reply, but Janet responded when we reached the counter. "No worse than you and Beck," she said with a roll of her eyes.

Maisie didn't even blush. "We're not as bad now that we have kids, and it's not nearly as romantic."

"Bullshit. That man can't keep his hands off of you, even at the station," Remy said with a chuckle.

We got our coffees and sandwiches, and Maisie hurried away to make it to the station on time while Remy walked me to my car. He carried a bag of sandwiches in one hand with a tray of coffees balanced atop that. He still managed to open my car door for me.

Once I buckled my seatbelt, he leaned down and fit his mouth over mine, his tongue sweeping inside. In a matter of seconds, our kiss was hot and heavy, and I forgot where we were until the sound of a car door slamming nearby snapped me out of it.

Kissing Remy was like diving into a fire, where everything around me disappeared into the heat and the flames. I kept thinking the feeling would fade. Maybe someday, it would. For now, I was noticing it was actually getting worse.

"Tonight," he murmured, his words a promise.

EPILOGUE

Rachel

Six months later

"Henry!" I called as he suddenly took off running. We were on one of my favorite trails for an afternoon run. The air had a bite to it, with summer over and autumn taking hold.

Autumn in Alaska was a blink—color exploding at your feet, and a dash of color fluttering through the sky before snow blanketed the landscape. Yellow and gold flashed in my periphery as I picked up my jog to a flat-out run. Lately, Henry had been doing much better about sticking with me when we were running on the trails, but he still had his moments.

Rounding a corner on the trail, my foot slipped on the damp leaves masking slightly muddy ground underneath. I fell down into the leaves, relieved I didn't hit anything hard. Looking ahead, I saw Remy standing there with Henry circling his legs.

"You could've let me know you were coming to meet us," I called.

Remy glanced up, and promptly stole my breath. Dear God. He was so damn sexy and handsome. Concern crossed his features as he strode toward me. With the sun angling through the trees as it dipped down along the horizon, gold glinted on his hair, casting his features into shadow.

He moved with an easy grace, his arms swinging and his shoulders outlined by his fitted T-shirt. He reached me, kneeling down at my side. "I didn't realize you were so close. You okay?"

"I'm fine, just a little muddy."

"Just a little muddy?" he asked, a grin stretching slowly across his face.

Remy's grins never failed to send butterflies spinning in my belly. He held a hand out. I reached up a muddy hand in return, warning, "You're gonna get mud all over you."

"That's quite all right, sweetheart," he replied as he tugged me up.

He pulled me straight into his arms, releasing my hand and sliding his palm down to cup my bottom. "I think I want to see a muddy print on that sweet ass," he murmured, right before he fit his mouth over mine.

There we were, in the middle of the woods, me with mud all over my back, and Remy kissing me, somehow making me feel as if I were the sexiest woman in the world.

He did that. All it took was a look, a touch, or a kiss.

Every.

Single.

Time.

By the time he drew back, I was barely able to stand, fire sliding through my veins and making my knees weak.

"I just came to see if you wanted to grab dinner tonight."

"You walked a half mile on the trail to see if I wanted to have dinner tonight?" I asked with a laugh.

He nodded. "Of course, sweetheart. I saw your car. I knew you two were going for a run this afternoon, and I didn't want to wait to see you."

"Do you mean dinner out?" At his nod, I smiled. "Of course. I need to shower first though."

"I'll join you for that," he murmured in reply. The gruff sound of his drawl never failed to make my heart beat a little faster.

He followed me home, *home* being his house now. Lately, he'd declared repeatedly that I needed to stop calling it *his* house and call it *our* house.

Remy tugged me into the shower with him when we got home. I couldn't say I'd thought much about it before—because I'd never been with a man who made me feel the way Remy did—but there was never a time when I didn't want him.

With steaming water pounding down around us, I found myself held in his arms, the cool tile pressing against my back as he sank inside of me, filling me in one deep surge. After he left me limp and sated from an explosive orgasm, I looked over as we were drying off, taking in the chiseled, cut lines of his muscles. Although my body was still tingling from the pleasure he'd sent spinning through me, I itched to touch him again already. Looking up, he caught my eye and winked.

"I think we should have dinner here," I said.

He tied the towel around his waist, his gaze considering. "Okay."

I couldn't say why, but I sensed something simmering under the surface with him. We'd settled into a comfortable routine with each other. All my worries after everything happened with Bruce had come to naught with Remy.

Speaking of Bruce, he'd left Willow Brook when I wasn't even paying attention. Rex had let me know. Even now, I couldn't describe the joy and relief I felt in realizing I had truly moved beyond the hold he had on me. The weight of fear I had carried was gone.

With Remy, everything was different. Being with him was easy. His strength was something I still leaned on. Yet, the gentleness that lay underneath was what defined him as a man. I savored his possessiveness, if only because I knew it came with no malice. It was simply that he was the man for me.

———

REMY

I meant to have it be an event, something special. But when Rachel said she wanted to have dinner at home, I couldn't say no. Hell, I couldn't say no to anything she asked.

Especially not when she was naked after her shower, her skin flushed pink all over from the steam. Most definitely not with the sharp memory of her slick pussy clenching around my cock only moments prior.

So, instead of over wine and candlelight, I proposed to her in our kitchen, with Henry snoring where he was sprawled out on the floor in the middle of the room.

"What?" she asked, her eyes widening.

"I hope you'll marry me," I repeated. "When you're ready." I paused, having to clear my throat to speak through the emotion catching in it. "I know, maybe..."

A tear rolled down her cheek, and she stood from where she was sitting on the stool across from me, hurrying around the counter and flinging her arms around me. I held her fast against me, feeling the *thud* of her heartbeat against mine. Leaning back, she cupped my cheeks in her hands and dusted kisses all over my face.

"You haven't answered," I said.

"Yes. Of course, yes," she said, becoming perfectly still in front of me. "There was never any doubt."

Another tear rolled down her cheek, and I lifted my thumb to brush it away. "What are those tears for?" I asked as concern tightened my chest.

"Those are happy tears," she replied with a smile.

"Happy tears? I don't like it when you cry."

She rolled her eyes, leaning forward to kiss me. When she drew back, her lips were a whisper away from mine. "I know you don't. I promise, those are good tears. You timed it perfectly."

"I did? I meant to take you out for dinner in Anchorage, but I couldn't say no when you said you wanted to have dinner here."

A wide smile stretched across her face. "Good thing I can't say no to you either."

"Why is it perfect?"

"Because I fell down in the mud today, and you helped me up. Just like last spring."

"I'll always help you up."

"I know."

Then, she was stepping between my knees and winding her arms around my neck. Every kiss reminded me again and again and again why loving her was worth the risk.

———

Thank you for reading Crash & Burn - I hope you loved Rachel & Remy's story!

I have a new series coming soon - squee! This Crazy Love will be the first book in the Swoon Series, coming in May 2019 - small town southern romance with enough heat to melt you! I promise you this series has plenty of alpha men with hearts of gold & sassy women who bring them to their knees!

Jackson & Shay's story is epic - steamy & intensely emotional. Jackson just happens to be Shay's brother's best friend. He's also *seriously* easy on the eyes. Shay has a past, the kind of past she would most definitely like to forget.

Past or not, Jackson is about to rock her world. Don't miss their story!

Keep reading for a sneak peek!

Be sure to sign up for my newsletter for the latest news, teasers & more! Click here to sign up: http:// jhcroixauthor.com/subscribe/

EXCERPT: THIS CRAZY LOVE

Shay

I climbed out of my car, wincing slightly as the door squeaked when I tried to shut it. With a little extra push, it closed all the way. My car was a bit like me. It was hanging in there, but it was rough around the edges. I was rather attached to it. In fact, lately, I felt more kindly toward my car than myself.

Before my thoughts meandered too far down that path—a well-worn rut of recrimination and regret—my attention was snagged by a small horse galloping across the pasture in front of me. The horse was almost black with three white feet, as if it were missing a sock. When I was a little girl, I had ridden horses for years and had missed being around them deeply.

The horse angled to the side, just enough for me to see its tail flick behind it and notice it was a male. The horse kicked its back feet up in the air and then turned to face the fence again. A white star stood out in the center of his forehead.

I was so absorbed in watching, I didn't quite notice what he was about to do until he came sailing over the fence in a

beautiful jump, the kind that would've gotten him a ribbon
in a show. Except we weren't in a show, and he'd just jumped
out of the pasture. The horse came running straight for me,
skidding to a stop before snorting and pawing at the ground.

Just as I was about to reach out, he spun around and
dashed off again, kicking dirt in my face.

"Mischief!" a voice called.

Sputtering, I dragged my sleeve across my face. Looking
ahead, I saw a man in the distance. A loud whistle followed
his call. I wondered if that was Jackson Stone. I wasn't close
enough to see from here. Whoever it was, he walked with an
easy strength and grace along the fence line.

Taking a deep breath, I glanced around. I'd left before
dawn this morning. A few hours of driving got me here just
as the sun was rising behind the mountains. The famous blue
haze over the Blue Ridge Mountains was shot through with
gold from the sun's early rays.

My gaze made its way back to the horse I presumed to
be Mischief. He slowed to a trot as the man approached
him and then came to a stop, docilely lowering his head as
the man slipped a halter on him. I watched as they turned
toward me again. It was a minute or so before they
reached me, but I recognized Jackson once he was close
enough.

I once had a bit of a crush on Jackson, years back.
Growing up, he'd been my brother's closest friend. He
remained one of Remy's best friends, even though they
didn't live anywhere near each other now.

With his shaggy brown curls and his piercing blue eyes, it
was fair to say I was not the only girl who had a crush on
him. I didn't think it was quite possible, but when he
stopped in front of me, he was somehow more sinfully handsome than he had been before.

He wore scuffed leather boots with jeans, and a black T-
shirt that didn't do much of anything to obscure the fact
that he had a body to die for, all muscle and hard planes.

Stopping in front of me, his mouth curled into a slow smile. "How's it going, Shay?"

"Aside from getting dirt kicked in my face, I'm fine," I said with a laugh.

Jackson's smile turned sheepish with a shrug. "Sorry 'bout that. Mischief lives up to his name." He glanced to the horse in question, giving him an affectionate rub under his chin. "Mischief, this is Shay, and she's a friend. So, be nice. He doesn't listen too well," he added with a glance to me.

As if he understood and to prove Jackson wrong, Mischief lifted his nose, gently nudging my shoulder with it. Despite teasing, I didn't really care about getting dirt kicked in my face. Dirt was the least of my worries. I lifted a hand and scratched between Mischief's ears, rewarded when he lowered his head and rubbed against my shoulder again.

When I looked back to Jackson, his blue gaze had darkened. A prickle ran up my spine, and I wondered if coming here had been the smartest move. Problem was, it was my only move. I didn't have any other good options.

I forced a smile and replied, "Well, he listens to you."

A grin stretched across Jackson's face, and my belly executed a little flip. Oh my.

"He listens when he wants and that's about it. Let me get him back in the pasture, and I'll take you inside."

I watched as Jackson strolled across the parking area toward the fence Mischief had just cleared in an easy jump, as if it was nothing more than a minor nuisance. Opening the gate, Jackson slipped his halter off and patted him on the rump as Mischief flicked his tail before trotting off to join a cluster of horses in the far corner of the pasture.

"Need help carrying anything inside?" Jackson asked as he stopped beside me.

His eyes traveled to my beat-up little hatchback. If he had an opinion about it, he stayed quiet. Once upon a time —which felt like forever ago at this point—I had a pretty good life.

I certainly had a car in better shape and enough money to get by. Now, I didn't want to tell anyone how much I needed this place to stay right now. I had *maybe* twenty-five bucks left in my bank account. Certainly not enough to get a new car, or cover any repairs. My little car was one of the few things that had seen me through both good and bad and was still chugging along, albeit a little banged up.

I watched Jackson's gaze coast over my car, hoping he didn't wonder about the dent just underneath the window in the driver's side door. A fist had left that behind. I didn't have the money to fix it and had learned insurance didn't cover people punching your car.

"Shay?" Jackson asked, his voice nudging me out of this ditch on memory lane, where I tended to get trapped.

"Oh right. I just have two bags," I replied quickly, finally springing into motion and striding over to my car.

Jackson insisted on carrying one of the bags, his fingers brushing mine and sending a hot little zing up my arm. I hadn't seen Jackson in five long years, but I'd never forgotten how handsome he was. Dear God, the man was swoon-worthy and then some. Yet, I didn't recall reacting this way to him before, even if I'd crushed on him a little when I was younger and shared a single, wild kiss one night.

That zing startled me. I had written off desire, figuring my life would be better off without it. I also figured I was pretty much ruined for it. That's what a few years of bad sex tangled up with fear could do. It made me question everything about desire and my own judgment.

As I looked ahead to the farmhouse, I reminded myself, rather sternly, I needed this to work out. I needed a place to regroup, and this was it. Even thinking about the sudden, confusing attraction to my brother's best friend was a *bad* idea.

JACKSON

Shay Martin had a mere two bags with her. "I can get one," she said, her tone a little testy when I moved to take both bags. Shay had always liked to do things for herself, so I let it go and turned with the one I already had in hand.

Moments later, we were inside the house. I led her through the sprawling farmhouse kitchen, down the hall, and up the stairs, going straight to the bedroom Ash had determined would be Shay's.

After our father passed away a few years ago, my sister and I inherited the family farm. Years back, it had been a working farm, with three generations of our family growing a variety of crops, including corn, tobacco, tomatoes, apples, and peaches. We still had the orchards, but that was all that was left when it came to farming.

In the last decade or so before our father passed away, he had wound down the farming part of it, and dedicated his time to his horses and creating an animal rescue sanctuary. Our mother had often taken in animals whenever someone asked her. Before she died, he promised her someday he'd make the farm a rescue.

Our father's death brought me home. With the rescue program entirely nonprofit, I'd followed Ash's lead with turning part of the property into an adventure lodge. We hosted a variety of guests throughout the year, with things slowing slightly in the winter months. We also opened up a veterinary clinic, seeing as I had my license, but I hadn't put it to much use while I'd been overseas in the military.

Ash was only here occasionally of late and was out of town now. She was one hundred percent on board with having Shay come stay here, so she made all the decisions about which room and so on.

Stopping by the door to the guest room in question, I glanced back to Shay. "Right in here," I said, pausing once I stepped inside and set her bag on the floor in front of the dresser.

When I looked over at Shay again, my breath was nearly knocked out of me. The early morning sunlight hadn't done her justice. If I thought she was beautiful before, she was arresting now. Her dark blonde hair fell in loose waves around her shoulders and almost reached her waist in the back. Her green eyes held mine as she looked at me, a hint of defiance entering her gaze.

Shay was on the short side and all curves. She wore fitted jeans and cowboy boots paired with a blouse. Even with her loose blouse, her breasts filled it, curves rising above the rounded neckline. Her lips were full and plump. She arched a brow as I looked at her.

"What?" she demanded.

I gave my head a little shake. "Not a thing. Ash will be thrilled to know you're here. You must have left early. Come on downstairs when you're ready. I'll take a quick shower and then I can show you around."

I walked through the door, ordering my body to ignore the sizzle of electricity in the air when I passed by her. It wasn't until I caught her gaze out of the corner of my eye, and saw the vulnerability under the defiance, that I remembered all the reasons why she was here.

"I'll be down in a little bit. I just want to unpack," she said.

I'd been up for hours and on my back in the dirt, changing the oil on one of the trucks. I needed a shower to clear my head as much as to get clean. I wondered if Shay was too close to my bedroom as I stepped through the doorway at an angle across the hallway. That was a problem for another day.

Coming Summer 2019!
   This Crazy Love

If you love steamy, small town romance, take a visit to
Diamond Creek, Alaska in my Last Frontier Lodge Series. A
sexy, alpha SEAL meets his match with a brainy heroine in
Take Me Home. It's FREE on all retailers! Don't miss Gage
& Marley's story!

Go here to sign up for information on new releases: http://
jhcroixauthor.com/subscribe/

FIND MY BOOKS

Thank you for reading Crash & Burn! I hope you enjoyed the story. If so, you can help other readers find my books in a variety of ways.

1) Write a review!
2) Sign up for my newsletter, so you can receive information about upcoming new releases & receive a FREE copy of one of my books: http://jhcroixauthor.com/subscribe/
3) Like and follow my Amazon Author page at https://amazon.com/author/jhcroix
4) Follow me on Bookbub at https://www.bookbub.com/authors/j-h-croix
5) Follow me on Twitter at https://twitter.com/JHCroix
6) Like my Facebook page at https://www.facebook.com/jhcroix

———

Into The Fire Series

Burn For Me
Slow Burn
Burn So Bad
Hot Mess
Burn So Good
Sweet Fire
Play With Fire
Melt With You
Burn For You
Crash & Burn
Brit Boys Sports Romance
The Play
Big Win
Out Of Bounds
Play Me
Naughty Wish
Diamond Creek Alaska Novels
When Love Comes
Follow Love
Love Unbroken
Love Untamed
Tumble Into Love
Christmas Nights
Last Frontier Lodge Novels
Take Me Home
Love at Last
Just This Once
Falling Fast
Stay With Me
When We Fall
Hold Me Close
Crazy For You
Catamount Lion Shifters
Protected Mate
Chosen Mate
Fated Mate

ACKNOWLEDGMENTS

To my readers for always asking for the next book. I can't adequately express just how much that means to me. Hugs to all of you.

My assistant, Erin T., has created an oasis of sanity and organization in my otherwise fly-by-the-seat-of-my-pants author world. Thank you for all of your help & for being so gracious stepping into my madness to tidy it up.

Much gratitude to Jenn Wood for helping me polish this story, and to Terri D. for her eagle eyed proofreading & for her support.

To my last line of defense, my proofreading angels - Janine, Beth P., Terri E., Heather H., & Carolyne B.

To DBC who is always there in every way. To my family for supporting my dreams. And to my dogs, because unconditional love is so pure.

xoxo
    J.H. Croix

ABOUT THE AUTHOR

USA Today Bestselling Author J. H. Croix lives in a small town in the historical farmlands of Maine with her husband and two spoiled dogs. Croix writes steamy contemporary romance with sassy women and alpha men who aren't afraid to show some emotion. Her love for quirky small-towns and the characters that inhabit them shines through in her writing. Take a walk on the wild side of romance with her bestselling novels!

Places you can find me:
jhcroixauthor.com
jhcroix@jhcroix.com

f facebook.com/jhcroix

🐦 twitter.com/jhcroix

⭕ instagram.com/jhcroix